ABOUT THE AUTHORS

Vishal S. Mahadkar (born November 30th, 1978) is a film director in the Indian Film Industry. Vishal has directed Blood Money (2012) for Vishesh Films. After Blood Money, Vishal wrote, directed and co-produced 3AM (2014).

Vishal grew up studying at renowned boarding schools like Sherwood College, in Nainital, and Dragon School in Oxford. Inspired by some of his experiences at school, Vishal penned down a film script called "The Fighter", set in boarding school. On reading it, his wife Tanvi suggested that this story be written as a novel too, and took on the responsibility of co-authoring this novel.

Tanvi Mahadkar, a copywriter by profession, has worked with some of the biggest advertising agencies in India like Law & Kenneth, DDB Mudra, Dentsu and Leo Burnett. Being a writer at heart, she was the best person to complement Vishal in writing this novel.

Disclaimer

This is a work of fiction. Names, characters, businesses, places, events and incidents are either the products of the author's imagination or used in a fictitious manner. Any resemblance to actual persons, living or dead, or actual events is purely coincidental.

Chapter 1

Sunday afternoon, March 1994, while most kids his age were still in bed watching reruns of *The Wonder Years*, Sahil Madhavan was showered and dressed to begin a new chapter in his life. While the technicalities of the divorce were still being worked out between his parents, Maneka and Sriram, they mutually decided that it would be best to send the 14 year old to a boarding school.

There he stood by the windowpane of his massive sea-facing apartment at Marine Drive, about to beat his highest score on Tetris – his favourite game. He showed neither anxiety, nor anticipation at the changes that were about to unfold in his life.

"Sahil, let's go, we'll be late...", called out a deep voice of a man. The 14 year old quickly put the Gameboy into the sling bag across his neck, and ran towards the door. Mr. Madhavan was in his early 40's, hair greying at the sides, but face still very youthful. He had a sense of calm that Sahil seemed to have inherited. With an old-school duffel bag on his shoulder, he dragged the suitcase out of the door. Pausing for a moment to look around the beautifully decorated house, he slammed the door shut. They walked out of the lobby, with Sahil almost running after him, trying to keep up.

He stood there in the lobby, breathing heavily as his old driver, Pyaareji, hurried towards him. Since his first day here, 13 years back, Pyaareji had been reporting to work wearing crisp white kurtas and pyjamas every single day. And today was no different. *"Good afternoon Sahil baba.* Saying this, he ushered Sahil towards the white Maruti Suzuki Esteem parked at the entrance. Mr Madhavan sat in the backseat while Sahil climbed into the front, next to the driver.

The 14 year old had always been a quiet boy who seemed to think more than he spoke, quite the opposite of boys his age. He spent most of his time in his room, reading Isaac Asimov or burying his head into his Gameboy - always beating his last Tetris or Super Mario score. In fact, when he wasn't buried in his Gameboy, he was turning his room into Mario world. Daydreaming was another hobby that he seemed to constantly get into trouble at school for. And he was at it again, just about to finish building an imaginary space shuttle for the ant sitting on the car's window, when the sudden jolt of the car brakes snapped him back to Pyaareji and Mr Madhavan's world. Pyaare had zipped all the way from Marine Drive to the Bombay domestic airport at Santacruz within a half hour. The next few hours to Nainital were a blur as Sahil slept through most of the journey. When he woke up in a luxury bus, he looked to his side and noticed the picturesque hillside through the window. Within minutes, a milestone passed by – *'Nainital 25 kms'*

Chapter 2

The winding road led up to the once Victorian, summer-escape town of Nainital. It looked as though the bus was gliding over a never-ending, white cottony blanket in the sky. It was a sight that would have left any other 14-year old mesmerised. But not Sahil. His face continued to remain as distant and emotionless as it had been through the journey. Even the breath-taking sights passing by, failed to distract him from the memories of his broken home some 1600 kilometres away. Just as he would start drifting into slumber, the bumpy roads would rudely jolt him back to the thoughts of his parents getting a divorce.

Lost in these thoughts, he dozed off again. As he slept, the innocence on his face matched the pure white clouds outside – untouched by the world. And yet, it exuded a quiet weariness of a grown man who had been through more twists and turns in life than this bus making its way through the Kumaon hills.

Loudly screeching to a halt after an 8-hour journey, the bus announced its arrival right in the middle of the quaint little town of Nainital. Sahil woke up blurry and rubbed his eyes before seeing an almost still lake glistening in the orange, setting sun. A number of shops that could very well be mistaken for tiny wooden huts surrounded the lake. The view, as Sahil could see, was right out of a postcard, but for some reason he felt it had a gloomy vibe too.

As Sahil got off the bus, he immediately started feeling his bag for his Kodak 110 pocket camera, thinking he would click a couple of photographs for his parents. Just then, an elderly man shouted out from across the street, *"O bhai! Shootcase upar leke jaaneka (sir, can I carry your suitcase)? "*. Startled, Sahil turned to look at him. He noticed a few others like him swarming around the passengers too. They were all coolies, dressed in soiled woollens, ready for a gruelling uphill trek. These guys looked 70, but actually weren't a day over 50. A hard life of labour, numbed by some 'charas' or 'tharra' had aged them by a few decades, turning their skin into a rough leathery texture. Each one of them carried around 4 trunks UPHILL, at least once every 30 minutes on busy days. The coolie that approached Sahil had just returned from one of the 3 km treks. Yet, without any hesitation or tiredness, he strutted ahead leaving the much younger Sahil stumbling behind him.

After a long walk along narrow, rubble trails, they had finally arrived. Even through the chilly foggy evening, Sahil was sweating and slightly dazed. He rubbed his eyes and saw huge gates with two words etched across them – *Oakwood College*.

At that moment, little did he know that these words were about to change his life forever. These two words were going to be the windows to the beauty of what life had to offer, and doorway to the beast within him.

Unfazed by the enormity of the gates, and the 'properness' of the brick stone structure that lay beyond, Sahil treaded on. Since he had enrolled in the middle of the term, he was the only admission at that time of the year. The coolie stopped at the gates and offloaded Sahil's suitcase on the dusty road. Sahil paid him the 5 rupees fee they had agreed on, which he promptly accepted before rushing off downhill. He was in a hurry to find the next "baksheesh" (tip) bearer of the day, after all.

Sahil watched on as the coolie left, realising for the first time that he was completely on his own. Just then, he checked for his Gameboy bag and held it tight, as if trying to grasp on to the only part of his 14 years of life that he was actually happy to have been left with.

Still clutching onto his Gameboy bag, with one hand, Sahil was standing there staring at the school facade. The school watchman, an old Nepali man came running and looked at the boy with his old, kind eyes before taking the bag from him.

Both of them quietly walked through the gates and were on their way to the school building. It seemed to be at least a kilometre away. But Sahil didn't mind the walk – it was a beautiful forest pathway with tall oak trees on both sides. He was enjoying the sound of the dried leaves crushing under his feet as much as the woody fragrance of the oak.

He had travelled to a lot of cold countries during his summers, growing up. But there was something very unique about the spring here in Nainital. There was a chill in the air and yet the setting sun was shining down at the same time, like a thin, warm, cosy blanket.

Just as the picturesque walkway came to an end, Sahil entered the front courtyard of the school. On his left, was a stonewall that came right up to his waist. One glance over the wall and he was swept off his feet. All he saw was a vast, never-ending expanse of the snow-capped Himalayas. They seemed to extend across the horizon before eventually ending at the foot of the Kumaon region. Sahil didn't know what heaven looked like, but decided instantly that it couldn't have been much different than what he was looking at. From where he was standing, the 14 year old was about 8000 feet above sea level and the thin air did something to his biochemistry that made him feel elated, almost euphoric.

Before Sahil was done soaking it all in, he had already arrived right in front of the Principal's Office. The Nepali watchman gestured him to go inside before leaving the suitcase at the doorway, and heading back to his station.

Chapter 3

As Sahil started walking towards the Principal's office, he noticed a bunch of students sitting around, in their green and grey uniforms. They were around his age, a little more muscular and a lot more thuggish. They started sizing him up like a pack of hungry wolves, waiting for their next prey: the newbie from Bombay.

"Stay calm." "Stay calm." he kept repeating the words in his head, while trying to make his way through their stares. The walk to the Principal's office from the courtyard seemed a lot longer than the one through the forest trail. This was the thing about Sahil. Unlike most kids his age, instead of being scared of being alone, he was uncomfortable being amongst people.

Pushing away the unwelcome thoughts and stares, he hurried into the Principal's office.

The principal, Mr Pontford, dressed in crisp grey trousers and a blue double-breasted blazer, looked every bit the title on his door. His moustache was impeccably British and hair was so slick that one would suspect he had a barber around him 24*7. Sahil immediately straightened his clothes, as if careful not to stand out through the perfect setting that Mr Pontford and his office were.

The principal noticed this as he was emptying his smoking pipe filled with ash, and smiled. *"Don't worry son, by the time you're out of Oakwood, you'll be every bit the man you have set out to be."* Saying this in his high baritone and perfect British accent, he got up and strolled outside, signalling Sahil to join him. As they stepped out and walked into the front courtyard, the boys had all dispersed and were doing their own thing. Or at least they were acting like they were!

Some of them were practicing basketball, others were playing chess and another one who seemed to be the comedian of the lot was cracking an audience up. They were all up to different things, but all of them looked like clones of each other with the uniforms and similar buzzed haircuts.

In his signature accent, the principal called out to one of them, *"Jatin Sethi"*

The Sardarji boy playing chess instantly got up and ran forward. Luckily, this one seemed a little less harmful than the others. In fact, he gave Sahil a pleasant smile that was diligently returned. The Principal continued, *"Sahil is new. Make him feel welcome at Oakwood."* Having said this, he walked away, giving the boy a chance to find his own space amongst the rest of the Oakwoodians.

Chapter 4

With a height of five feet and eight inches at the age of 14, Jatin Sethi was one of the taller kids in the class. This automatically made him the backbencher, and hence, one of the naughtiest. Even then, there was something very kind about him. He was born to a upper middle-class, educated Sikh parents that hailed from a humble village in Ludhiana. His grandpa was a journalist who had started his own paper delivery shop about 80 years back, during the British rule. This shop, now run by Jatin's father and uncles, had grown into the no.1 paper delivery business in Ludhiana.

Jatin was naughty in a very endearing kind of way. He was the perfect balance of book smart and street sharp, which made him a favourite with the teachers. The brash bigger kids bullied him in jest, but loved him. However, he preferred keeping a low profile, something very out of character for a Punjabi.

Jatin, or 'Sethi' as he was fondly known, made small talk with Sahil. He walked him through the corridors of the school building, the sports ground, etc. briefing him along the way.

Sensing that the newcomer couldn't care less about the school's architecture or teachers that he was talking about, Jatin cut short his briefing session, *"You know what bro, let's get you to the canteen first where we can order your uniforms and your monthly supplies."*

Sahil just nodded his head. Sethi was slightly frustrated by his don't give-a-damn demeanour, but realised that he was just an introvert. In fact he gauged that Sahil was probably even low, and the first day of being in an alien place with alien people wasn't the best setting to get him in his element.

As they made their way to the canteen, they passed by a group of boys about the same age as them. They alternated between looking towards Sahil and talking amongst themselves and guffawing loudly. He knew the joke was on him, or rather all the jokes were on him. After all, he was the odd one out. And not being in uniform made it easier for them to spot him.

His thought bubble was quickly burst by a small rock that he stumbled upon. Now even more aware of the fact that he was the only one dressed in casuals, he felt more naked than ever!

Sethi helped Sahil up, before discreetly pointing to a stout scruffy boy amongst the group. He started murmuring something to the newcomer as if filling him in on a top secret of the school:

"That's Caesar. He is in our class but has flunked twice. Everyone suspects he does it purposely because he just enjoys bossing around the rest of the juniors in class. His cousin is Rudra, our headboy, so no one messes with him. If you ever need any grub and you have the cash, Caesar is your man. Next to him, is his gang... Anurag, Namit, Shivdasani, Goldy, Anoop and Mann. You might not remember their names, just remember not to mess with them."

They walked past Caesar and his gang standing at the canteen's entrance. In the canteen, Sethi helped Sahil place an order for his uniform along with completing the rest of the formalities. After Sahil was done giving his measurements, he was issued his roll number "423".

Sethi told him to remember his roll number as that would be his first name in school. Second would be Sahil.

Just then a senior called out to them, *"Hey idiots!"*

Chapter 5

Infuriated at the choice of words, both turned back. The angry scowls on their faces quickly changed to nervousness as they saw a tall, well-built Nepali boy with a vicious, menacing look on his face. He looked a couple of years older than them. Something, or rather everything about him blared 'Don't mess with me'.

Jatin snapped out of his frozen moment and quickly acknowledged with a couple of quick nods. He pulled Sahil with him towards the burly boy.
On the way, he whispered, *"That's Rana, our house prefect."*

Before he could give any more information, Rana started ragging Sahil with embarrassing questions.

His voice resonated with arrogance, *"What's your name, chotu (little guy)?"*

The 'chotu' reference never went down too well with Sahil. For someone who had experienced more life than most others his age, the 14 year old considered the words to be an insult.

Sahil replied, trying hard to conceal his anger, *"Sahil Madhavan"*

Rana sensed the irritation and raised the arrogance in his voice a couple of notches, just to aggravate the guy. *"Roll number?"*

Sahil stared at the ground.

Rana, *"Now chotu, I don't have all day to waste here."*

Sahil looked at Jatin who was staring back at him. He even gestured Sahil something that he gathered as 'respond or you're going to be dead'. Sahil mumbled his fresh new roll number through his clenched teeth, *"423"*. He didn't think he'd have to use it till the next morning in class.

Rana snapped, *"You messing with me? Are you a bloody retard? Speak clearly, what the hell is your roll number?"*

Sahil looked up at Rana and replied, *"423."*

The sadist that Rana was, he started enjoying this. *"So, 423, how come your parents haven't come to drop you? Don't they love your sorry ass?"*

Sahil held his gaze, not trying to conceal the rage in his eyes anymore.

"Oh! Looks like I've pissed you off huh. What happened chotu? Don't you have any parents? Maybe you don't, maybe you're a bastard!"

Sahil had had enough. The big temper that this little guy had pent up, finally gave way. He snapped back at Rana, oblivious to the repercussions of back answering a senior at Oakwood. And this one wasn't just any senior. He was the Godfather of them all.

By now, a few other students had gathered around, each eager to see how this was going to end.

Sahil replied with a straight gaze, *"Maybe you're the bloody bastard."*

Jaws dropped to the floor and mouths were left ajar. Especially Jatin who suddenly saw the meek newcomer transform into a completely different person, felt part nervous part proud. Unfortunately though, at that moment, Rana was feeling a completely contradictory set of emotions. He was stunned by the display of guts by the scrawny 5 feet 5 inches 'chotu'. But more than that, he became aware of the crowd gathered around, watching him get publicly humiliated. That too by a 14 year old who had just walked in a few hours ago. He immediately went into prefect mode.

Before Sahil knew it, Rana had struck a hard blow across his face. It hit him like lightning, before snapping him right out of his adrenaline-pumped alter ego that had taken over a few seconds ago. Sahil fell to the floor, now trembling with fear and pain. He felt a sharp sting inside his nose, followed by a gush of fresh blood that started uncontrollably running down his lips to his chin, and onto the floor.

He hadn't even close to recovered from this blow, when Rana knocked another violent punch into his ear. Everything around him went quiet, barring a screeching sound that echoed through his entire body. Then, the prefect mercilessly pounded another blow into Sahil's bloody face, and then another. This continued till the 14 year old slipped out of consciousness.

The last thing Sahil noticed before he blacked out was Tina, a pretty girl watching him from a distance. She had a worried look on her face.

Finally, interrupting the avalanche of kicks and blows, Jatin came forward and pleaded Rana to stop. *"Forget it Rana, let him go. He is new and doesn't know the ways yet."*

After a couple more kicks, Rana seemed satisfied by the damage he had done. He stopped beating Sahil who was lying there lifeless, and warned Jatin, *"You better teach him real quick, Sethi. Teach him how to respect his seniors, because the next time I won't be so lenient."* Having said this, he spat on the floor next to Sahil before walking off. The rest of his entourage scrambled behind him.

Sahil suddenly felt like he had been thrown into an ice-cold swimming pool. He woke up gasping, as Jatin splashed water on his face. Sahil panicked as he saw strange faces all around staring down at him. He wasn't sure if he was having a dream or if any of this was real. That's when he noticed Jatin in the crowd and got his bearings back. He was now aware of where he was and how he had gotten there.

Jatin pulled up the badly bruised Sahil, and supported him as he staggered to the dorm. The crowd quietly began to disperse, only talking in whispers about the 'exciting' day that had just unfolded. Caesar and his gang too, had watched the entire drama. However, they walked away casually like they had gotten out of a movie theatre, satisfied with the entertainment they had received for the day.

Chapter 6

Jatin helped Sahil up and supported him as he limped through the sea of dumbfounded students, whispering amongst each other. Everyone else was too scared to help. No one was ready to risk getting on Rana's wrong side.

Jatin took Sahil to the dorms to get away from very public humiliation that had just been inflicted upon him. He felt bad for the boy who was still shaken up. As Jatin wiped Sahil's bloody nose on a kerchief, he gave him some very important advice, *"Sahil, you can't back answer seniors here. Treat them like you would a God and you'll be fine. Remember, that's the unspoken law here."*

Jatin consoled Sahil and decided to get his mind off of things by introducing him to the other dorm-mates. He met them all, but not surprisingly, was still preoccupied with what had just happened. An experience like that on your first day at school could take a while to get over.

However, their cheerful demeanour did comfort the boy a little. And he went from wanting to bury himself in a hole to just burying his face into the pillow on his bed. Soon, the fatigue set in and he fell asleep face down into his pillow. After what seemed like only a few minutes, Jatin woke him up, *"It's time for dinner. Don't you want to go wash up before we go down."*

Still groggy, Sahil got out of bed and noticed his bedside locker. He realised that it had his roll number "423" on it.

The number immediately brought back fresh memories from a few hours back, and Rana's words echoed in his ears... *"So, 423, how come your parents haven't come to drop you? Don't they love your sorry ass?"*

Chapter 7

While everyone else went ahead for dinner, Sahil decided to stay in the dorm. He told Jatin he wasn't really hungry, when the truth was that he was too tired to deal with the embarrassment of being the 'poor boy' who got beaten up on his first day at school.

It was night and the other boys were back from dinner. Jatin had also sneaked in a banana for Sahil, which he gobbled up in seconds. He then sat in bed fiddling with his Gameboy. Some of the boys were just chitchatting amongst themselves, about some girl they liked in class. The others were in their night suits, getting ready for bed.

Right then, a prefect walked in and yelled, "LIGHTS OUT!" Suddenly everybody scampered off to their beds like rats into their holes. Jatin was right; every senior was somewhat of a God out here at Oakwood College. Within seconds, there was pin drop silence in the entire dorm.

Sahil was sitting on his bed, ignorant of all that had been happening around him all this while. The other boys gossiping, the prefect's 'Light's Out' order, the scramble to get into bed, it was all a blur for the teenager who was too busy trying to make sense of the curveballs that life was tirelessly throwing at him. And now, he had gotten too tired – to keep fighting them back, or even to keep shielding himself from them.

After the lights went out, the moonlight cut a peaceful, sage-like silhouette of him. But the state of his mind, raging with anger and disappointment, was completely the opposite. He had thought the fight between his parents had taught him to deal with any kind of violence that came his way. But the punch that was thrown at him a few hours back, had proved otherwise. He was angry at himself, for how weak he felt at that very moment.

His eyes filled with tears. Suddenly, he broke down and started weeping unstoppably. He cried hard, muffling the sudden sobs with his pillow, careful not to make a sound. He crawled into a foetal position and continued to weep and weep and weep, till he realised it was already dawn. The outburst had left him tired and sleep deprived. But in some strange way, it had also helped him feel lighter. He needed this.

And now, he was actually looking forward to finding out whether Oakwood College had anything in store for him, other than the very forgettable first day?

Chapter 8

Sahil had just about settled into deep slumber when the deafeningly shrill 6 am bell jolted him out of his bed. As he opened his eyes, he noticed all the others around him running from one end of the dormitory to another. It looked like a mass exodus of sorts.

As Sahil stepped out of his bed, he almost got tripped over by a boy racing to the bathroom. Jatin and his gang had already showered and were now getting ready in a military-like drill. Hooking the pants while putting on the shirt, and combing the hair while trying the get the tie perfect.

Sahil was trying to make sense of all this panic around him, when Jatin yelled across the dorm, *"Dude Sahil! Hurry up and get ready. We only have 10 minutes to be down."* Sahil heard this and started scrambling for his toiletries from his bag.

He rushed to the bathroom, which looked like yet another battlefield with boys running in and out of showers, shoving out anyone who came in their way. Sahil spotted the sink and pushed right through till he managed to secure himself a good spot. He felt victorious about his little achievement. As he was trying to brush his teeth, the other, more seasoned kids pushed him around trying to get the prime real estate of the sink for themselves. However, he managed to get out of there in a single piece.

For any new student at Oakwood College, the first few weeks were the most daunting during their time here. The morning had taken Sahil back to some of the jail films he had watched. He felt like the new inmate, whereas others around were the seasoned thugs who knew their way around prison. And in a lot of ways, he was right. From getting the biggest shower cubicle to securing the best spot at the sink – here, it was the rule of the jungle and survival of the strongest.

Challenge 1 had been accomplished. He had successfully brushed without getting trampled in the stampede. It was now time for Challenge 2: Getting a shower cubicle. Sahil raced right up to the cubicle that was at the farthest end from the lockers. He was the 8th boy in the queue, which wasn't so bad compared to the queues at the other cubicles.

Finally done with his morning rituals, Sahil strolled into the dorm in his bathrobe. The rush had settled. Infact the dorm was empty sparing a bunch of kids who ran out as he walked in, and Jatin. He was ready too, but was waiting for Sahil. He knew that after what had happened yesterday, if he would have left Sahil on his own this morning, he would either have not turned up to class, run away from school or done something worse.

Even though Sahil seemed to be in a shell after all the attempts by Jatin to break the ice, the latter felt very protective, almost elder brotherly towards him.

As soon as Jatin saw him, he threw a uniform shirt at Sahil while pushing him to buck up. Jatin's voice was clouded with urgency and panic as he spoke, *"Dude what the hell! We don't have all the time in the world. We are damn late, get ready fast. We are the last ones here!"*

Sahil wore his shirt, hurried into his pants and combed his hair back. He stumbled over himself while trying to get his socks on his feet. He finally wore his shoes, and turned around to see the mess he had created – towel on the floor, toiletries scattered on the bed, etc. and was contemplating clearing it up. Right at that moment, Jatin yelled out from the dorm door, *"Bro lets go or we're dead!"* They rushed out, with Sahil trying to tuck his shirt in on the way. He couldn't understand what was the big deal with being a few minutes late.

This was always the case with newbies. They underestimated the importance of being at the morning assembly on time.

Chapter 9

The two boys dashed across the corridors of the dormitory. The early morning breeze skimmed through Sahil's wet hair as he ran across the courtyard. They finally reached the front of the courtyard where the rest of the school had gathered. It was a sea of 600 hundred odd students, all freshly showered, neatly dressed and gathered up in formation with their hands behind, standing at ease. There was dead silence except for the wind rustling leaves on a tree, almost like a background track to the single student who was reciting the morning student brief. It was one of the seniors, Rudra – immaculately dressed, with a composed and confident posture. He was in Class 12, and was the College Captain (head boy) of the school.

Just when the brief was about to end, Jatin and Sahil ran to join the queue closest to them. Their attempt to make the entry as inconspicuous as they could was in vain, as the students in the assembly turned around to give them amazed looks. They all wanted to see who was to be the 'unlucky one' for the day, about to be subjected to the merciless punishment whetted out by the prefects. When they realised one of them was Sahil, the new boy who had taken on Rana on his very first day, they all looked a little concerned.

The head boy noticed them. As soon as he finished the brief, he called them towards him. Standing next to him was Rana as were all the other senior prefects. At this moment, Sahil wanted to run in the opposite direction, out of the school gates and on the next bus back to Bombay.

Rudra spoke in the same confident voice that echoed during the brief,
"You two are late."

Jatin immediately went on to clarify for the both of them. *"I'm sorry Rudra, it's his first day and I was helping him."*

Rudra, *"Ok, make sure it doesn't happen again. Rana, take care of this. Everyone except 9th standard is dismissed."*

The entire school broke formation and as if in unison, started walking towards the dining hall. Once again, Sahil was reminded of a jail movie where the inmates moved around in herds, blindly following orders of the prison guard. Questions and resistance were crimes that were dealt with very, very strictly, as Sahil had learnt the previous day.

Even Rudra walked off with the other prefects into the dining hall, leaving the boys with Rana.

Rana's face lit up like a Christmas tree as he looked at Sahil. "*My my my.. must be my lucky day. You guys seem to be just asking for it haan...*"

He now turned his attention towards the rest of the batch.

Rana, "*You boys do know that if any one student is late, the whole batch is punished right?*"

On hearing this, one of the students, Caesar, shook his head in disbelief and clenched his jaws. Caesar looked at least a couple of years older than his classmates, and his uniform was giving way at its seams.

As Rana continued to speak, he spoke while alternating between a smirk and a scowl. It made him look uglier than he already was.

Rana, "*However, even though I would really love to make you guys pee in you pants right now, this is the first time. So being as kind as I am, I shall let you'll off with the first and final warning. Next time, it will be your asses and my trusted hockey stick. Now everyone is dismissed, double time to the dining hall!*"

After saying this, he patted Sahil on his cheek and walked off. Everyone ran to the dining hall while Sahil was still staring at the ground in front of him. Jatin nudged him out of his trance, and they both followed everyone else.

Chapter 10

The dining hall was bustling with students talking amongst themselves, interspersed by the clinking of cutlery on steel plates. They were all seated across long dining tables, each with plates, quarter plates and cutlery laid out before them. The bearers (servers) all dressed in similar uniforms, queued up for the tables. While one started serving slices of bread to the students, another spooned out blobs of scrambled egg into their plates. Another came along with trolley of bananas, one for every student.

Sahil was famished. The last proper meal he had eaten was back home in Bombay. The sight of food reminded him of how hungry he was. As soon as the bread was served, Sahil greedily picked a slice and went for his first bite, when Jatin smacked his hand. The bread fell right back into the plate. Sahil looked at Jatin, bewildered.

"You are playing with fire dude! The food in this school is dangerous. It can bite back. Here... watch and learn." Jatin, very seriously explained to Sahil.

He held the bread slice up against the light, like a scientist studying some new specimen. Sahil could almost see through the translucent slice of bread. There were some dark patches on it that Jatin carefully picked out and held in his palm, for Sahil to see. The newcomer watched in disbelief as he saw that the dark patches were nothing but grey worms wriggling amongst each other in the piece of bread that Jatin had picked.

"You can eat it now!", he casually told Sahil who had lost all his appetite by now, and was still staring at the slice. Jatin on the other hand, went back to eating non-chalantly, like this was a daily pre-breakfast ritual.

Sahil ditched the bread and turned his attention the blob of scrambled egg that was served to him. He was still mustering up the courage to take a bite of the scrambled egg, trying hard not to imagine what surprises he would find in it. Just then, somebody pushed Sahil from behind. It was Caesar, trying to squeeze in next to Jatin and him.

Sahil noticed his plate, topped with 6-7 slices of bread and at least a few helpings of the scrambled egg. As Caesar took a big bite of the bread, Sahil couldn't help but imagine all the protein (in the form of worms) that he was ingesting. Caesar was a loud eater, not to mention an obnoxious one too.

As he stuffed his mouth with the egg, he started talking to Sahil, "*Listen shithead, I know you are new and all, but if I have to go through any fatigues (punishments) because of you, it's going to be hell for you. You hear me, don't you bloody be late again. Or its me you'll have to worry about, not the prefects!*"

Having said this, he got up and gave Sahil a dead stare before knocking over his teacup. It nearly spilled on the terrified 14 year old, as he watched Caesar walk off.

Sahil was convinced. This was a prison in a school's guise. Since he had walked in, less than 24 hours back, he had already been threatened thrice! Every school had bullies. But these weren't bullies, they were thugs who didn't mind some blood on their hands just to get their points across. He was daydreaming again, one of the gangster movies he had watched playing in his head. All the actors were replaced by Rana, Caesar and the others that he had met so far.

The school bell almost shattered his eardrums before it snapped him out of his imaginary world. As he resurfaced, he noticed a stampede-like situation in the dining hall. Hundreds of students were falling over each other to get to their respective classes. Sahil panicked as he knew he couldn't afford another goof-up. All of a sudden, he dashed through all the kids, making his way to the entrance. Realising he had left Jatin behind, Sahil turned back to see him looking amused at the sudden burst of energy.

Chapter 11

After a lot of struggled manoeuvring through the throng of students, Sahil successfully made it to the classroom on time. For the first time since he had entered Oakwood, he didn't feel like a complete stranger. The old-world British charm, the teakwood benches and desks, the wooden clock hanging off the wall, it all seemed way too familiar. He was teleported back to the era of the British Raj that his grandfather described in all his stories.

The teacher was already in class, and blended perfectly with the classic British setting. She looked like she was around 65 years old. The delicate wrinkles on her face made her look wise and endearing, all at once. Her soft silver-grey hair didn't have even a hint of dye. It was the mark of a confident woman who was courageous enough to age gracefully. Mrs Pontford had been the English teacher at Oakwood for the past 30 years. Her simple yet elegant dressing, with a grey pencil skirt, collared peach blouse and a simple string of pearls, spoke volumes of her position and seniority at this school.

Mrs Pontford was putting down some pointers on the blackboard as the students streamed in. Sahil settled into one of the few empty desks and looked around. He saw Tina and immediately recognised her from the previous day. It was the same smile that he had managed to remember from the moments before Rana had beat him out of consciousness. She was holding a textbook but her mind was wandering. Her gaze was fixed on Sahil. She smiled shyly at him as soon as he looked her way, as if waiting for him to notice her. He smiled back. Both of them were so busy with this exchange that neither noticed that the class had already begun. Luckily, the teacher's back was towards the students as she was meticulously writing something on the board. Jatin nudged Sahil, breaking him and Tina from their moment.

Up until then, Sahil hadn't even noticed Jatin come into class and join him at his desk. He had been a little too busy playing smiley face with the mystery girl.

Jatin whispered, *"Dude! That's Tina, Rana's ex-girlfriend. She's trouble man, stay away."* Before Jatin could say anymore, the two boys were interrupted by a piece of chalk that flew right between their faces. They looked up, startled, and noticed their English teacher who was about to throw another piece at them.

They ducked to save themselves from the projectile, when she stopped.

"Mr Jatin Sethi, kindly share with the whole class the very important conversation you were just having!"

Although it seemed like a request, the sternness in her voice made it clear it wasn't.

Jatin was trying to rack his brain for a good excuse, *"Nothing ma'am, I was just telling Sahil here, which page we were on."*

Sahil was now a little worried, as it would have been a record-breaking number of times that he had gotten himself into trouble in the last 24 hours.

Mrs. Pontford, voice still stern, turned her attention to Sahil, *"Ohh, I see. And you sir, stand up."*

Sahil slowly stood up, reluctantly. His feet felt wobbly as he noticed the rest of the class staring right at him.

"What's your name? You are new right?" Mrs. Pontford asked.

Sahil cleared his throat and finally found his voice, *"Sir...errr... I mean ma'am, I'm Sahil Madhavan. Uhh yes, I just joined yesterday."*

Mrs. Pontford sounded irritated, *"Ok Sahil, since you are a little lost with our textbook, let me see what you have learnt in your previous school. Did you study Julius Caesar in English literature?"*

Sahil felt slightly more confident as he answered, *"Yes Ma'am, I did."*

Mrs. Pontford replied, *"Ok, kindly recite his famous speech."*

"Friends, Romans, countrymen....umm", Sahil started reciting the speech, unsure and nervous. But as the words started rolling out, he seemed to get more and more confident, finally reaching the dramatic flair of a professional theatre actor. Mrs. Pontford who started off angered by the boy, had now started enjoying Sahil's narration. She had a sparkle in her eyes as she was impressed by his recital. This command over language and expression had

become increasingly rare amongst children through her years of teaching. Finally when Sahil finished, Mrs. Pontford put on a poker face, concealing the fact that she was thoroughly impressed.

She retreated to her previous strict demeanour as she finally spoke, *"Not bad Mr. Sahil Madhavan. Now if you only pay attention in my class, maybe you will learn some more."*

As she finished her sentence, the class bell rang loudly, marking the end of that period.

Mrs. Pontford started gathering her books as she gave the students an assignment, *"Saved by the bell! Class I want you'll to complete exercise 4 on page 26 for prep."*

The class unanimously started whispering amongst each other. Some panicked while the others started cribbing about the assignment.

Unaffected by the reaction, Mrs. Pontford walked out of the classroom. As she left, Sahil heaved a sigh of relief that he hadn't gotten himself into any serious trouble. He looked around class and noticed Tina watching him. She smiled at him playfully.

Once again, Jatin attempted to nip this little love story in the bud, before it began. He didn't want the problem child to get into any more trouble with the seniors than he already was. And 'Tina' only meant trouble!

Jatin interrupted, *"Hey Sahil! What sport do you play?"* Before Sahil could reply, he continued, *"There's a friendly inter-house football match happening tomorrow. Come, play with us."* Saying this, he jumped over his desk to a group of boys.

Most of them were 5'10" or more. Jatin spoke to them as Sahil stood back. After a few minutes, he signalled the newcomer to come over. As he walked over to them, Sahil noticed a couple of the boys were from the dormitory. Jatin introduced him to each of them. It was nice to finally have met people who actually spoke to him instead of threatening him. After some small talk, the boys packed up to leave class. As they walked out, they invited Sahil to play on their team in the next day's match.

Chapter 12

It was a sunny morning. The nip in the air made it perfect weather for an outdoorsy day. That day, Sahil dealt with the morning routine much better than he had on his first. After getting ready, he headed out to the sports field along with Jatin. As they stood at the entrance of the gravelled flat expanse, Sahil took a moment to soak in the enormity that lay ahead of him. Where he came from, that much space was a luxury not even the best schools in town could afford. The entire field was divided into 4 basketball and 2 football fields. This was the one place in the entire school where students of different classes and divisions came together.

It was a half kilometre walk from the front courtyard to the football field where their game was about to take place. As soon as both the boys got there, the others greeted them with high fives before quickly getting into a team huddle. One of the players briefed Sahil on the opponents' strengths and weaknesses. Although he forgot their names almost instantly, Sahil remembered each one of them by their positions on the field.

All the players got into position. A sports teacher who was refereeing, placed the ball in the centre before blowing a loud whistle. The match had begun. Caesar was playing for the opposition team, and kicked off the game with the ball. After he passed it to a fellow teammate, the battle for the ball began. The guys from the other team were much bigger and taller. However, they all knew, on field nothing mattered except the focus. A few minutes into the game, the ball was passed back to Caesar. He dribbled and carefully maneuvered it across the field, to the defence of the other team. Sahil was playing defence.

The seating area was already filled with audience for this interclass game. There were also a few girls cheering loudly for one of the two teams. Most of them were girlfriends of the players. Tina was amongst them too.

As Sahil noticed Caesar dribbling towards him, he jumped into action. The latest entrant on the field ran towards Caesar, tackled him and cleared the ball, all in a fraction of a second. As the audience witnessed this rare sight, the cheering suddenly stopped. Caesar was known as the 'King of the Field' after all, and no one had managed to tackle him so effortlessly before. The pin drop silence in the audience stand was interrupted by an enthusiastic Tina, who suddenly started clapping and cheering at the top of her voice. Caesar seemed visibly furious as he pushed Sahil away and ran to the other end of the field, where the ball was.

Not wanting to be defeated at any cost, Caesar charged at the ball like a bull that had seen red. The game went on for a while before Caesar finally got hold of it. Determined to score a goal this time, he dribbled back towards the post. As he saw Sahil inch closer to him, he could see Tina cheering loudly in the background. He clenched his teeth tight, and like a hungry lion going after his prey, tripped Sahil over. Immediately, the teacher refereeing blew the whistle. It was a fowl and Sahil had just won himself a free kick. He cleared the ball again. Still determined, Caesar ran and claimed the ball back. This time, he dribbled through all the players and came towards Sahil with full force. Tina started cheering even louder for Sahil, who turned to look towards her for exactly a split second. Caesar noticed this and ceased the opportunity to mock pass the ball, confusing Sahil. And then he swiftly dribbled past him and scored a goal. The referee blew the whistle signalling the end of the match. Caesar's team had won. They all rushed to him, giving him high fives as Sahil looked at his own team that seemed disappointed. They started walking away, defeated. Even Tina and the girls looked upset and they got up, dusted their uniforms and walked away. The field was almost empty as Sahil bent down and started taking off his gear. Trying to take in his defeat, he was disappointed with himself for getting distracted at such a crucial moment in the game. Suddenly he saw a shadow approaching him and before he could turn around to see who or what it was, he was pushed over. It was Caesar who had pushed him, causing him to fall to the dusty ground. He then showed Sahil the middle finger. Caesar's friends guffawed at this action as all of them walked away. Sahil looked on, tired and defeated.

He wondered if this constant feeling of defeat and humiliation would ever go away or would he have to live with it through his time here at Oakwood. It wasn't getting any easier for Sahil, the boarding school life. He felt angry with his parents for having thrown him into this big bad ocean that he was only sinking into. He knew that the only reason he was here today was because his parents didn't want him to witness their divorce. He often wondered, wouldn't it be easier for them to just forgive each other and go back to being a normal happy family? Shaking these thoughts off, along with the mud that had gotten onto his uniform, Sahil got up. He started walking towards the entrance of the sports field where he saw Jatin talking to the other team members. On the way, flashes of Tina's face and voice as she cheered for him from the audience, kept appearing. And then suddenly Jatin's voice echoed with the advice he had tried to give Sahil in the classroom, "*That's Tina, Rana's ex girlfriend... she's trouble man, stay away...*" This advice pretty much fell on deaf ears as Sahil saw her standing with her gang, next to Jatin and the other teammates. As Sahil walked out of the entrance, she turned to look at him before giving him that smile he had become familiar with. Their moment was once again interrupted by none other than Jatin. "*Let's go for lunch bro! The dining hall will shut soon and we still have to change.*" Even the other teammates joined them. The rest of the mealtime was spent discussing the game, next time's strategy and player positions.

Chapter 13

As they finished lunch, the bell for the next class rang. Sahil, Jatin and the rest of the teammates rushed to their classroom. The geometry teacher was already in, drawing up diagrams on the board. The boys made it to their respective desks, trying to catch their breath as they brought out their textbooks. The other students were already in, settled and bored. One of them was holding an Archie comic within the textbook, pretending to study. The other was carving his name onto the desk with a divider. And the remaining were trying very hard to stay awake.

Tina, who was in class too, seemed more distracted than the others. She folded a piece of paper and quietly sneaked it to the guy on the neighbouring bench, the one engrossed in his comic. The note said "Sahil". In a hurry to get back to his Archies, he passed it on to the next student, who passed it on to the next. And so on.

In today's world, we see students constantly communicating with each other through SMS, Facebook, Whatsapp and what not. But back in 1994, the only way to send a message across a classroom was by passing it through half a class of students before it reached the desired recipient.

The note finally reached Sahil who was almost dozing off thanks to the deadly combination of the afternoon lunch mixed with Geometry theorems. The neighbouring student nudged him awake and discreetly passed it to him, careful that the teacher doesn't see.

Sahil opened the note, as he looked around, a little confused. As he saw whom it was from, he covertly slipped it between his textbook pages before continuing to read it. He then quickly crumpled it and put it in his pocket. Jatin noticed this, and as soon as the bell rang, he paced towards Sahil. However, Sahil hurriedly left the classroom before Jatin could even get to him.

Chapter 14

Jatin dashed out of the classroom, in an attempt to catch up with Sahil. When he spotted him in the front courtyard, standing by himself, Jatin hurriedly started making his way towards Sahil. But before he could make it, he saw Tina walk up to him and hold out her hand as they shook hands. Jatin stopped dead in his tracks, not knowing how to react, or which way to turn. Sahil was about to get himself into a lot of trouble, and Jatin wanted to drill that into his head before it was too late. But he realised, that it probably was way too late.

While the two chitchatted, Tina's group of friends was standing in a corner, giggling away as they looked on. She heard them and turned around to signal them to go away. Sahil noticed that she was as tall as him, maybe even slightly taller, and was suddenly aware of how beautiful and slender she was.

Tina suddenly turned back, and flashed that smile of hers once again...the one that had distracted Sahil and cost him a victory during his football match. He was now embarrassed as he knew she had caught him staring at her.

"We haven't officially met yet. I'm Tina.", she said as Sahil shook her hand, in an unsure manner.

"Sahil...", too busy blushing, all Sahil could manage was his two-syllable name.

Tina was absolutely at ease, and in fact enjoying working up Sahil's nerves a little bit. She continued, *"You played well this afternoon."*

Uncomfortable with the praise, Sahil replied, *"I tried..."*

Tina, *"No, you were good. Really!"*

As she flashed her magnetic smile again, Sahil, who was just beginning to relax, went back to his initial nervous self. He replied, *"Yep..."*

Tina was smiling playfully now, *"Sahil, you sure are the talkative types!!! Walk me to the girl's hostel?"*

Before she could complete her question, Sahil jumped in, "*Yes, yes! Absolutely!*"

Tina let out a giggle at his enthusiasm, kissed him on the cheek and grabbed his arm, leading the way. Sahil was doing backflips and cartwheels in his head, but all he did in reality was sheepishly follow her. As they walked away, both of them were absolutely unaware that the entire class had been watching them. Jatin who was also one of the spectators, noticed the crowd and shook his head in worry. He knew then, that in the next half hour, this piece of gossip was going to be the talking point of Oakwood. At this school, even if a single person witnessed something like today, it was the hot topic for the next few weeks. Here, the events had unfolded in full view of an entire class.

Chapter 15

Adjoining every dorm was a 100-sq.foot cubicle aka "cubes" that was home to all sorts of devious activity. Two prefects assigned to each batch of juniors shared one such cube. The purpose of this practice was to maintain law and order in every dorm, outside of class hours. However, first day ragging sessions or day-to-day punishments for the juniors, or senior meets on important topics, were some of the less controversial operations that took place here. Other than operating out of this space for these activities, it also doubled up as the living quarters for the 2 seniors. Officially it had 2 beds, 2 bedside tables and 2 cupboards. The cupboards were there to store all the confiscated goods that were banned on campus. But the prefects would come in and redo the rooms to their liking, with things like music systems, lamps, heating coils for late night Maggi cravings made in mugs, fancy car and Samantha Fox posters, family pictures, etc.

None of the students dared to venture into this 'prefects' cubicle' unless they were summoned as victims of the next fatigue (punishment) session, or were invited as audience to witness others being ragged or punished. The latter however, only happened if one belonged to the prefects' coveted inner sanctum.

It was one of the usual 4 pm sessions being held at the prefects' cubicle, which was also called 'The Den'. A junior was sitting in a 'murga' (chicken) position as Rana chatted away with a fellow prefect friend, enjoying cigarettes and Thumbs Up. There were chocolates and other foodstuff surrounding them, probably confiscated from some poor juniors. There was another junior running around the two prefects, serving them, lighting their cigarettes, and even polishing their shoes. The ecosystem of this place seemed pretty organised with everyone around clear about who the bosses were and who the menials were.

Suddenly Luthra, one of the juniors from Caesar's gang dashed in. Trying to catch his breath, he almost stumbled over the two juniors, interrupting the conversation between the prefects.

Rana immediately dismissed all the other juniors and without wasting any time, he turned to Luthra, *"Bolo narad muni… Kya khabar laye ho?(tell me, what news do you have today)"*

Luthra replied, with visible distress over his sweaty face, *"Its not good news boss... It's Tina.. Sahil's been hanging out with her.. He's gone now to drop her to the girls' hostel..."*

Rana, without flinching replied, *"I see... Good job Luthra. Here..."* Saying this, he tossed over a couple of bars of chocolate to him. Luthra, who seemed pleased with himself and his little reward, ran right off.

If Rana was feeling any rage right now, he did a very good job of hiding it. However, anyone who knew anything about the guy, would know that he was already strategizing how to make Sahil's life hell. The newbie hadn't just picked a battle with any prefect, he had picked it with the most vicious, cruel, ruthless one of them all.

Chapter 16

The next morning, the entire school gathered in the front courtyard as usual. This time Jatin and Sahil were on time too, and already standing in the assembly. Sahil, although facing forward, kept looking at Tina who was standing two rows away in the girls' line. From the corner of her eye, she noticed him too and gave him a sideway glance before flashing her magnetic smile once again. Both of them were oblivious to the students around them, who were noticing their little flirtation. Rudra, the headboy, who adjusted the mike to begin the brief, finally managed to distract them. Soon the daily brief was done and the school dismissed. Everyone started walking towards the dining hall for their breakfast including Sahil and Jatin. They had barely walked a few steps when Rana stopped them.

Rana paced around them, sizing them up as he spoke. *"I see that you'll were on time today. Unfortunately, you aren't wearing regulation black shoes. That's a violation roll number 423."* Saying this, he pointed at Sahil's white sneakers that had turned brown with dust after the football match.

Sahil argued back, *"But I don't have black shoes yet."*

Rana, who always looked forward to these little conversations with the new juniors, seemed to be particularly enjoying this one. He replied with something between a smile and a scowl, *"Not my problem chotu... Jatin, get your entire class to meet me after dinner today."*

Having made himself clear, Rana walked away leaving the two boys staring blankly at him. Jatin knew what this was all about and didn't look pleased. *"I told you not to mess with Tina man. Now we're screwed!"*

Sahil looked a little embarrassed as he replied, *"Dude, what am I supposed to do? I like her man."*

Sahil's reply got Jatin even more worked up, as he shot back, *"What? Just after 1 day of knowing her? Whatever dude."*

Saying this, he walked off to the dining hall, leaving Sahil behind.

Sahil was terrified about being in the face of danger ONCE AGAIN. But he was secretly enjoying this feeling of fear mixed with taboo. Watching Tina giggling with her friends about some secret girly joke in the dining hall, only made things more exciting. It's funny how hormones can turn an otherwise shy teenage boy into thinking of himself as a superhero who feels he can conquer the world, even if past experiences have taught him otherwise.

Sahil was snapped out of his fantasyland again by the sharp reverberation of the school bell that he had no clue, was right next to him. It was the final call announcing that breakfast was being served. Sahil rushed into the dining hall, trying to find Jatin. He was sitting at the usual place they sat at everyday, with some of the guys from the football match. He looked preoccupied and didn't even notice when Sahil walked in. Sahil engaged in random conversation with the rest of them, while gobbling down his breakfast of scrambled eggs and toast. Before leaving the table, Jatin announced to everyone in general that Rana had asked the class to regroup at the front courtyard after school.

Chapter 17

That day, Sahil and Jatin went through most classes without exchanging more than a few words. Jatin, who was visibly miffed at Sahil, was only thinking about what Rana was about to come up with. The newcomer, however, was too distracted by the doe-eyed Tina to worry about what Rana had in store for them that evening.

The last period for the day was prep class. The students were all writing letters home. Sahil was sitting at his desk, staring at a blank piece of paper with 'Dear Dad...' scribbled in it. After a long thoughtful pause, he decided to put down all about his new life at Oakwood. He never admitted it even to himself, but like every 14 year old, all Sahil wanted was for his dad to be proud of him just for once. And he thought writing about the timetable, the morning regime and the discipline was something that his dad would enjoy reading about, given his military background. Out of everything Oakwood had thrown at him, Sahil was happy that it had given him the chance to have something to talk about with his father. Of course, there were some less than pleasant details that he made sure to leave out.

The class monitor collected all the envelopes with the letters, sealed, stamped and ready for the postman. The bell rang, marking the end of yet another school day. Sahil had forgotten all about the after-class meeting that Rana had summoned, until he saw him standing right outside their classroom door. He walked into class and made an announcement for all the boys to assemble in formation in the front courtyard immediately. The boys exchanged worried glances amongst each other, without saying a word. Sahil too, could now feel the sense of panic creeping in. What was it going to be this time?

As the boys ran out, Tina and the other girls from the class looked on, concerned.

Rana was pacing impatiently up and down the courtyard, with a hockey stick in his hand, waiting for the boys to take their positions. Once they were settled, Rana wasted no time as he started talking. "*So boys, get ready for a fun night. Roll number 423 here hasn't been wearing regulation shoes. So I think its time to remind you all of the regulations. Get down and give me 50 push ups.*"

As soon as he said this, the boys wasted no time jumping straight to the ground. Well aware of the deadly repercussions, did they not follow the orders immediately, they started doing the push ups. Sahil too followed the rest and did as was commanded. By the time they reached the 50th one, they were scrambling over themselves, gasping for breath and ready to collapse. Then, Rana mercilessly shouted out, *"50 frog jumps!"* and the boys went from the ground, straight onto two feet. Within seconds, 35 boys were doing frog jumps making the front courtyard look and sound like a furious bison herd. The girls, who were helplessly watching the boys being punished, now started walking away. Sahil wasn't as upset about the punishment as he was humiliated about the fact that Tina was watching them get punished.

The boys were sapped out of every ounce of energy in their bodies, but none of them dared to stop. They knew the rules too well. Anyone slacking in the fatigues (punishment) was made to bend down, as Rana brutally swung his hockey stick in full force onto their butts. This was probably the most common punishment amongst Oakwoodians for years and had now turned into a tradition. The prefect would angle his hockey stick like a golf club, and deliver a full-armed swing onto the butt cheeks of the junior being punished, always leaving a black and blue mark in the shape of the Nike logo. In fact this fatigue was famously called the 'Nike tick' as a joke amongst the ones who had experienced it, which included almost every Oakwoodian.

If an outsider were to walk into the school right now, it would look like a rigorous commando training camp rather than a high school. The punishments these 14 year olds were being subjected to, were the kind that made grown men quit and flee from military school.

Just when it looked like Rana was satisfied with the punishments he had meted, he instructed them to do continuous summersaults across the front courtyard. The boys angrily glanced at Sahil, as they obeyed the prefect's command. Finally after about an hour of army-drill punishments, commonly known as fatigues, Rana told them to stand back in line. They looked like they were going to faint any moment, some of them even trembling out of muscle exhaustion.

Rana walked around swinging his hockey stick, as he spoke to the class.

He sounded pleased with the hell that he had put class 9 through, as he spoke, "*So boys, I hope this has been as much fun for you as it has been for me. You have your new friend Mr. Sahil Madhavan to thank for this. I hope you make sure he knows regulation uniform from now on. Have a good night boys. Now up to you beds and lights out in exactly one minute!*"

As soon as he said this, the boys dispersed. They ran to their dorms like it was a matter of life-and-death. Sahil, who felt sick with exhaustion followed suit.

Chapter 18

Once the boys were in the dorms, they started changing
hurriedly. There was no time to shower or wash up after those
punishments in the dusty courtyard. The boys just about
managed to change from their soiled uniforms into night suits.

Caesar was right next to Sahil, as they changed quickly into their
nightwear. He gave him a scornful look before mumbling off a
warning to him, *"You're so dead."*

They promptly jumped into their respective beds, and the lights
were switched off. Luckily, each student was allowed a bottle of
water on his bedside, that there were no time restrictions on
when one could drink it.

A few minutes after lights out, Sahil sat back up in bed and
glugged down his entire bottle of water before falling back in bed.
He was exhausted and just like everyone else, fell asleep almost
instantly.

Chapter 19

Tired from the previous night's punishments, most of the boys overslept the next day, especially Sahil, for whom this gruesome version of an "exercise regime" was a first. Jatin finally shook him out of his slumber and pushed him into the bathroom to get ready for the day. They just about made it in time for the morning assembly.

The rest of the day dragged by with the entire class quieter than usual. They were all sore and fatigued, and couldn't wait for the day to end. It was finally the last class for the day – Mrs. Pontford's English session. The students were already in class when the teacher walked in with a broad smile on her face. She had a bundle of marked test papers in her hands. As soon as she reached her desk, Mrs. Pontford plonked the papers on it. While the rest of them were tied up in that bundle, there was one test paper lying loose on top. It had red ticks all over it. Mrs. Pontford proudly picked it, looked at it and kept it aside. She quickly distributed the rest of the test papers, commenting on a few along the way. Once she was done, everyone but Sahil had received their corrected papers. He knew he had 'pissed her off' in the last class, and she was planning detention, or punishment or some other form of humiliation of some kind. Finally, Mrs. Pontford picked the loose paper that she had set aside on the table with the bright red ticks.

She looked at Sahil, with a glimmer in her eyes as she spoke, *"Looks like I underestimated you Mr. Madhavan. You have scored the highest in your first test. In fact none of your classmates even came close to you. I am particularly impressed with your correct usage of grammar and rich vocabulary. Keep it up son."*

After hearing this, Sahil was in shock. He wasn't used to this. Appreciation and encouragement! From his time here at Oakwood, he had come to understand that appreciation was too out of character for anyone here, let alone a senior teacher. He was snapped out of his thoughts by Mrs. Pontford shouting out from her desk, *"Sahil"*. He went up to collect his paper and carefully scanned it. "Not bad", he thought. For the first time since he had set foot in Oakwood, at least there was one thing he had done right. On the way back to his desk, he quickly glanced at Tina to see her reaction. But she was looking straight ahead at the teacher.

Retreating to her stern demeanour, Mrs. Pontford addressed the class. "*The rest of you should learn something from him and buck up.*" Having said this, she shot a sharp look at Caesar through her rimless spectacles. She was just about done discussing the results of the test papers, when the class bell rang.

Mrs. Pontford started packing up, as she assigned the class their study work for the weekend, "*I want you all to have a good weekend and read pages 15 to 25 of your textbooks for the next class.*"

As soon as she was done with her announcement, the students started leaving the class. It was the last class for the week, and everyone, especially the boys had looked forward to this moment through the day. Some of them were even limping thanks to the previous night's punishment.

Even Tina, who otherwise would have lingered around for a while with her girl friends or at least exchanged a smile with Sahil, hurriedly left the class. She didn't seem in her usual element. Sahil noticed this, and got up to leave so he could catch up with her. Throughout class that day, he had kept wondering if there was something he had said or done on their walk to her hostel that might have angered her. He replayed the entire time in his mind, over and over again. He couldn't put a finger on what it was that he had done to upset her, but he was about to find out. However, as soon as he started walking out of class, Sahil tripped over something and fell. As he got up, he saw Caesar grinning, sitting with his leg stretched out. Sahil realised that he had deliberately tripped him and was outraged. But in light of everything that had transpired between him and others here at Oakwood in the past few days, Sahil consciously decided to stay out of trouble – at least for now.

Mrs. Pontford, however, noticed Sahil fall just as she was about to leave class. She hurried back in and asked him if he was ok. Caesar immediately pulled his outstretched leg back and looked away, acting completely unaware of what had just happened.

Sahil, who was slightly embarrassed, replied that he was just fine. He went on to explain that he must have tripped over the desk leg. Just then Jatin gave Sahil a hand up, and they quickly walked out of the class after Mrs. Pontford.

Chapter 20

Jatin and Sahil walked out of the classroom together, but Sahil paced ahead to catch up with Tina. Suddenly he saw something and stopped dead in his tracks. His face was flushed red with shock and anger; he couldn't believe what he saw in the front courtyard.

Tina was at the far end with Rana, under the same tree that she was with Sahil two days ago. She was giggling and laughing, and the two seemed to be having a good time as they were chatting away. Seeing this made Sahil furious. His eyes were glazed, and he clenched his jaws. Even if Tina noticed him there, she seemed completely unfazed and carried on with her little rendezvous with the prefect. Caesar, who walked out of class soon after, saw this and let out a snotty laugh before walking away. Jatin saw how upset Sahil was and tried to comfort him by patting his shoulder.

Sahil pushed Jatin's hand away, and starts walking towards Tina and Rana. His eyes were red with anger and disappointment, and his male ego had taken over all reason. He was a few yards away from the couple, when he was suddenly held by the arm and pulled away into an adjoining corridor. It was Julie, one of Tina's friends. Sahil had seen her around the campus and in class, but had never spoken to her.

Julie had the voice of a little girl. The pleading tone in her voice as she spoke to Sahil, made her sound even more innocent and child-like, *"Stop Sahil! You'll make a fool of yourself."*

Sahil replied, still staring at Tina and Rana from the corridor, *"What the hell do you mean? What are you talking about?"*

Julie turned Sahil's face towards her, as she spoke, *"Tina never liked you Sahil."*

At this moment, Sahil was stunned and didn't know how to react. He didn't want to believe what he was hearing, as he retaliated, *"What bullshit? You girls just make shit up. You're just insecure."*

Julie ignored Sahil's immature accusation and pleaded with him to forget about Tina. She went on to explain to a reluctant and hurt Sahil, what Tina's flirtation with him had been all about. *"Sahil, she was just using you to get her ex-boyfriend Rana jealous, so he would get back with her. You were just a part of her strategy. And as you can see, it has worked."*

No matter how badly Sahil wanted to term this as lies and bullshit, he knew it was true. There was no better explanation to Tina's behaviour. He was left heart broken and speechless. Julie walked away, letting Sahil have his own space to mourn the end of his short-lived romance. After all, at 14 even a two-day long infatuation can feel like a case of true love, leaving the victim devastated, depressed and even suicidal.

Back in the dorm that evening, Jatin made small talk with Sahil, trying to distract him from yet another eventful day. He asked Sahil, *"Your first heartbreak bro?"* Sahil didn't reply. Tina wasn't just the first one to break his heart; she was the first girl that Sahil ever had had more than a one-minute conversation with.

Jatin who had been through a few failed relationships himself, knew that Sahil would get over this one. He also knew that more than a wounded heart, it was a wounded ego that Sahil was nursing. Sahil, however, felt differently. He was distraught, depressed and kept to himself for the rest of the evening. In the dorm, there were others who had seen what had happened today, and had found their hot gossip for the day. Sahil heard some of the boys murmuring about today's incident amongst themselves. But he chose to ignore them and started getting ready for bed instead.

Despite Jatin and his gang's insistence, Sahil decided to skip dinner and turn in early that night. As he lay in bed, flashes of Tina and Rana getting close in the courtyard kept him up. He was still angry with her for making a fool out of him. The truth was, he was angrier with himself for letting her make a fool out of him.

Chapter 21

The next day was a Sunday, and there was no morning assembly. The students were allowed to wake up at 7 am instead of 6.30, and directly show up for breakfast at 8.

Sahil was sitting at the dining table, fiddling with his very watery porridge. While most of the others on the table had almost finished their breakfast, he was still playing with the spoon in his bowl. Even through the chaotic dining hall, bustling with chatter and clinking and students stomping in and out, all he could hear were Julie's words – *"She used you to get back with Rana."*

Jatin noticed that Sahil was still low and tried to make conversation. *"Bro, we have to start practicing for basketball too. Sports day is coming up, and this time we need to kick the opponent's ass."* Caesar, who was sitting a few tables away, had just finished his breakfast. He saw Sahil and Jatin, and couldn't stop himself from walking over to their table for his day's fix of entertainment. One of the quiet, lanky guys from class was sitting on the chair right across Sahil. As soon as Caesar came up behind his chair, he jumped up and scooted away. The hefty teenager sat right in front of Sahil and started making small talk with Mann, one of the guys from his group. Unable to resist the temptation to pick on Sahil for barely 30 seconds, Caesar started cracking jokes about how Tina had used the newcomer. Sahil tried to ignore the first few nasty comments in order to avoid any drama, till something finally snapped inside him.

Suddenly, Sahil took one powerful lunge across the table and started punching Caesar with full force. The entire steel table shook and the porridge bowls on it flew in different directions. Luckily, everyone else on the ill-fated table was done with their breakfast. As soon as they recovered from what had just happened, the rest of the crowd leapt out of their seats and moved away from the table. Caesar, too, was stunned by Sahil's sudden attack. But he managed to compose himself before pulling the skinny 14 year old from across the table, by his collar. Caesar's chair tumbled back causing the two to fall down to the ground. They started brawling in the dining hall, exchanging punch after punch for the next minute or so. By now, instead of commotion, the entire dining hall had broken into a curious silence. They had gathered around the two boys, each trying to get the best view of the fight that was unfolding.

Jatin tried to stop the two from fighting, but got a hard blow on his mouth in the process. Finally, all the classmates came together, trying to separate the two before either seriously injured the other.

At that very moment, Rana who had just received the news of this fight, walked into the dining hall. He made his way through the very crowded dining hall, and saw that the two were still at it. He watched for a few seconds and suddenly kicked them both in the backs, one after the other. Sahil and Caesar finally let go of each other. Both of them were badly bruised with blood flowing out of their noses. Their uniform shirt buttons had been ripped off and hair, dishevelled.

Rana yelled, "*Both of you get up right now.*"

Both Sahil and Caesar stood up, realising the kind of trouble they were in.

Rana continued, "*So, you'll enjoy fighting haan? Come here!*"

He pulled the two by their tattered shirts, and made them stand opposite each other. This was the moment both of them realised that they were in clear view of the entire school. Neither knew what was coming, but they knew that each and every student there was going to watch them go through the humiliation.

Rana, "*Let's see how tough you guys really are. Caesar slap Sahil. Come on give it to him.*"

Caesar was a little confused by Rana's order, but went ahead and slapped Sahil. However, he didn't do it too hard.

Rana looked at Caesar with disgust as he shouted out, "*Stop slapping like a bloody girl and slap him hard, I want the whole school to hear it. Sahil started the fight right? He hit you right? Take your revenge!*"

On hearing this, Caesar got all charged up. He went for a full swing slap across Sahil's face. It was so hard, it almost knocked the teenager over. The entire school was startled by the sound that the slap made. Tears welled up in Sahil's eyes as the warm blood came gushing to his cheek, along with a sudden stinging pain. He held the side of his face, which went completely red and felt like it was on fire, with imprints of Caesar's palm on it. Somehow, Sahil managed to recover from the shock, making sure he does not fall.

Caesar now had a victorious grin across his face. He felt proud about what Rana had let him do. It most definitely meant that the senior was ready to make him a part of his infamous crew.

Rana was quick to burst his bubble, as he started speaking again, *"That's more like it. Now Sahil, bloody show him what you are made of. It's your turn, slap him hard!"*

No sooner did Sahil hear this, he took a full-forced swing across Caesar's face, causing him to fall onto one of the dining tables next to them. The impact was so strong, it caused the dining table to cave in. Caesar immediately got up despite the numbing blow he had just received.

Rana then instructed Caesar to slap Sahil again, and Caesar did. This time, it felt like a thunderbolt had struck from the sky. Sahil didn't know what had hit him, and fell down. However, the adrenaline that was now rushing through his body, wasn't about to let him give up just yet. He sprung back up on his feet, and heard Rana instructing him to slap Caesar once again. Sahil was now mentally in one of the WWF fights that he loved watching as a kid. Rana was the coach, and the rest of the students looked like real audience. He could also hear them cheer behind him.

This slapping match went on, till the pain and tiredness caught up. The slaps kept getting lighter and lighter, till both of them eventually stopped. Rana and his friends, who were watching and enjoying the fun, had a good laugh and finally let them off.

Rana, *"Boys I can't tell you how much I have enjoyed this. Anyway, why don't you'll rest for a bit and I'll meet you tonight in your dorms before dinner. Let's continue the party then, shall we. School Dismissed."*

Saying this, he and his friends left the dining hall. The other students too started leaving. Sahil and Caesar were standing there, both in an equally bad state, with swollen and bruised faces, looking at each other. What seemed like hours of battling it out with each other, had in actuality lasted for just three minutes.

Chapter 22

The long, eventful day was finally over. Sahil and Caesar walked into their dorms, without exchanging any smart jibes or vengeful looks. They were both too sore thanks to the slapping competition that Rana had thrown them into. Any more violence would have been too much to handle for a day, even for a seasoned Oakwoodian like Caesar.

Sahil headed straight to the dorm bathroom. The guy staring back at him from the mirror looked like a distorted damaged version of himself. His face had swollen up and Caesar's slaps had left bright red impressions that had already started to turn blackish blue. As soon as Sahil splashed cold tap water on his face, it stung like bees from an entire hive had attacked it. He braved the pain and kept splashing the water till it began to soothe down the burning sensation instead of stinging.

It was half an hour before bedtime. All the boys had changed and were sitting in their respective beds, waiting for Rana. There was silence across the dorm. They all looked anxious, but Sahil and Caesar were especially quiet. Both knew that they were in for some sadistic punishment from Rana. Sahil nervously tapped his fingers on the side of his bed, trying to mentally prepare himself for the worst. Was it going to be a ridiculous number of push-ups? Or another round of violent kicks and punches? Or was it going to be something more unimaginable, more disgraceful?

Two juniors who walked in with huge cloth bags, and stood right at the dorm entrance interrupted Sahil's thoughts. Caesar looked on worried, expecting more company but not knowing what else to expect. Soon, Rana walked in with two other prefect buddies. Sahil and Caesar, both jumped out of their beds on seeing them and stood in attention. Rana noticed their swollen faces and let out a lopsided, unapologetic smile. He enjoyed having control over these boys, and before them, many others who had fallen prey to his dreaded punishments.

Rana, "*You know I was thinking about you guys and I felt really bad for you'll. I mean look at your faces...*"

He continued to talk as he examined Sahil's swollen and bruised face in his hand firmly, causing a pricking sensation to pass through it, *"I have decided to take it easy on you and so I have an easy punishment for you all."*

Saying this, Rana snapped his fingers with the flair of a seasoned stage actor. The two juniors standing behind him promptly emptied the bags that they were holding, onto the floor. Both of them were in sync like a pair of robots, as they offloaded a pile of soiled socks and dirty underwear.

Once they were done, Rana looked at the two boys with a satisfied smile across his face. *"It's the weekend, so here's something special for you'll. I want all these socks and undies washed by morning. They belong to us, the 12th standard batch. So make sure they are clean and put them out to dry in the drying room. I don't want a single one lost!"*

Rana's friends started guffawing at the plight of the poor boys. Rana joined in too, till the entire dorm started echoing with evil, monstrous laughter. The rest of the dorm pitied the two boys, but at the same time heaved a sigh of relief that it wasn't the rest of them going through the punishments too. Jatin wanted to help Sahil, but he knew better than that. He had been at Oakwood long enough to know that getting yourself involved in someone else's fatigues meant definite hell for you in the form of unforgiving punishments, with double the intensity. Soon as the prefects stopped laughing, the entire dorm was back to its previous pin drop silent self.

Without a sign of trepidation or guilt, the seniors walked out of the dorm. Rana joined his buddies, but not before he shot Caesar and Sahil a sharp, merciless look before grunting out, *"Enjoy the weekend ladies."*

Chapter 23

Only a few minutes after the seniors had left, did the boys dare to move from their positions. They started talking amongst each other, discussing the day's incident as they prepared their beds. Sahil and Caesar quietly went on to inspect the piles of socks and underwear that had been left for them on the floor. Sahil could smell the stench of the dirty laundry even from a distance, and immediately wanted to throw up. He held his breath and quickly gathered one of the piles into a bag, before heading to the bathroom. Caesar too, who had been through the nastiest punishments in his 4 years here, hadn't experienced one like this.

Soon, it was 'lights out' for everyone else in the dorm. Sahil and Caesar looked at each other as they walked into the bathroom. Without exchanging a word, both threw the disgusting clothing on the floor next to them and started with the washing at their respective washbasins. Neither of them spoke for the next 3 hours, as they scrubbed the grime and soil off every sock and underwear that came their way. Both of them were covered in filthy brown foam as they continued washing away. All Sahil hoped was for this ordeal of the worst kind to end without getting sick. It was around 1.20 am, and the two finally had just a few dirty undies and socks to go.

Caesar tried to wipe some of the foam away from his swollen cheek, as a sharp sting made him jump in pain. He squealed, "*Damn... man, why did you have to hit so hard. It bloody hurts!*"

Sahil was taken aback by Caesar's sudden mood for conversation, but did not waste any time replying. He looked at Caesar through the mirror and answered, "*You did too man. Look at my bloody face.*"

Caesar, "*Yeah but I didn't know you had such a heavy hand man, I mean it really hurts now.*"

Sahil, "*You too dude, I'm in pain as well, from your slaps... and from all the stench of these dirty socks!*"

Both of them broke into laughter at their own sorry state. Strangely, in some weird way, their showdown had given Sahil and Caesar the feeling of having been through something together. They both continued with their washing, trying their best to get this ordeal over with as quickly as possible.

Caesar washed his last pair of underwear as he spoke, *"But dude, I have to say, you fought well. Like a real man."*

Having said this, he extended his foamy hand out for a shake. Sahil didn't mind, as he went for the handshake enthusiastically, instantly ending weeks of animosity and hatred. However, was this going to be a longstanding friendship or just a 'partner-in-misery' case? That was something they both would have to wait and find out.

Caesar waited for Sahil to finish washing his last few pairs of socks, before both of them headed to the drying area to finish the most disgusting task of their lives. As they put the clean laundry out to dry, they joked about Sahil's first few weeks at Oakwood, the football match and Tina. And Sahil didn't seem to mind, even as Caesar pulled his leg about how Tina had broken his heart.

In fact, Sahil was surprised at how joking about it actually didn't make him sad at all. It made him feel better, and made him realise that he had already moved on from his little heartbreak. Caesar too, shared his first experiences at Oakwood with Sahil – first love, first punishment, first fight... the newcomer took it all in, like a child hearing a bedtime story for the first time. It made him feel better that he wasn't the only victim to Oakwood's quirky ways of welcoming its newcomers.

This was fun. This was the first time he had really had a real conversation since he had walked into this school.

Chapter 24

The previous night had tired both the boys out. They woke up groggy and worn out from the gruelling laundry session. Sahil sat in bed, rubbing his eyes, when he realised that he wasn't done with the punishment yet. He still had to fold all the dried out laundry and arrange it back in the bag. He glanced at Caesar's bed, and realised he was already up and probably done with folding up his share of the socks and undies.

Sahil ran to the bathroom and saw Caesar. He had finished folding his own laundry and half of Sahil's too. Pleasantly surprised as well as confused by this gesture, Sahil walked up to the drying area. Caesar saw him and tossed over the pair of undies he was folding. *"All yours bro! Hurry up or you're going to be in for another round of fatigues."* Caesar ran off to get ready for the day, and within no time, Sahil was done with his part of the folding too. He hurried through the rest of his morning rituals, turned in the 'finally clean' laundry at Rana's cubicle and made it just in time for the assembly. The rest of the day went comparatively smoothly, a welcome change from the last few eventful days.

At dinner, Sahil sat with the usual suspects – Jatin and the basketball group. Caesar walked in with his gang too, and joined them. This was the beginning of a brand new friendship at Oakwood.

The onlookers were surprised at this sudden camaraderie between the two. Just yesterday these boys were at each other's throats. And today, here they were together, breaking bread. But then this was how most teenage experiences were – friendships, love, rivalries, nothing was permanent.

The next few weeks went fairly smooth for Sahil. His flair and command over the English language was much appreciated by Mrs. Pontford. Soon she started mentoring him for various upcoming essay and elocution competitions, and the two developed a great mentor-mentee relationship. Infact not just English but other subjects' teachers too saw the spark in Sahil. Soon he was one of the star students of that batch. He often helped his teachers, especially Mrs. Pontford, by taking the books to and from the staffroom.

On one such visit to the staffroom, he noticed the large ventilators above the window. They were left wide open, without any grill or barricade to secure it, irrespective of whether the staffroom was locked or not. *"Cookies?"*, Mrs. Pontford had distracted him from his next thought by offering him a butter cookie from the secret booty in her desk's lower drawer.

Sahil and Caesar had become an inseparable duo, and were also known amongst their friends as the 'A' team. Even in sports, they would team up to play and ended up dominating most of the wins. Caesar introduced Sahil to the underground world of Oakwood's food and alcohol black market. At first, Sahil was shocked and even hesitant to get involved. But at the age of 14, the lure of adventure and excitement can be so blinding, it easily blurs the line between right and wrong. Entering the 'high school mafia' had Sahil mingling with the who's who of Oakwood's senior batches. He even started getting closer to the headboy Rudra who was the don of this entire black trade.

Foodstuff that was prohibited in school premises like Coke cans, chips, chocolates, was also known as 'tuck'. And like prohibited goods anywhere else in the world, even at Oakwood, this tuck was traded at a good price amongst the students. Whenever someone got back from holiday, they would get back foodstuff, which would all get confiscated. However, if they bribed the prefects with a part of the goodies, they got to keep the rest of it. At Oakwood, 'tuck' was the unofficial currency. You could buy alcohol, exam papers and even cigarettes with it. And guess what? The students weren't the only ones involved in this well-oiled black market. Nainital city had a popular family-run kirana store called 'Bhutani General Stores' who were hand-in-glove with these students too. The workers here would buy alcohol from the local wine shop and keep it hidden away at the store. Whenever the Oakwood boys came down to the market during the weekend, they would buy the alcohol bottles from these workers.

The students not involved in these activities usually stayed miles away from those who were, even at school. That included Jatin and the rest of his group. They stayed away from the likes of Caesar and his gang.

However, after the fight and the consequent friendship between Caesar and Sahil, something had changed remarkably. For the first time in the history of Oakwood, a batch wasn't divided into smaller cliques. For the first time, each and every one from the entire batch – right from frontbenchers to last-benchers, miscreants to star students, had come together as a single unit. The entire batch was now one single team.

Chapter 25

At the end of dinner one day, Caesar murmured something in Sahil's ears as if letting him in on a top secret. It was an invitation to hang out with him and his gang at their undercover location – "the roof". Sahil had no idea that an accessible dorm roof even existed, but gladly accepted the invite. Caesar gave Sahil specific instructions on how to get there and left the dining hall.

"First, wait for lights out. Then, all you have to do is climb out the dorm window. On the left, you'll see a drainage pipe. Hold on to it and swing to the tin roof on top of it. The roof is angled at almost 45 degree angle, so you'll have to run up to the flat patch before you lose balance." When Sahil heard these directions, he wondered if they led to a real place? Or was it just Caesar playing a prank on him? And if it was a real place, why hadn't he heard about it yet from even a single person so far? Either way, he wanted to find out.

Once he got back from dinner, he went about his end-of-day regime, got into bed and waited for 'lights out' as usual. Once the lights were off, hardly ten minutes later, he heard the ruffle of blankets. As he strained his eyes, he noticed some movement across the dorm. He saw some shadows move towards the dorm window. The next thing he knew, some boys were climbing out of the window one after the other. Once the last boy was out, Sahil walked to the window mumbling to himself, *"Climb out the dorm window, to the left..."* As he looked out to his left, he stood there stunned for a few seconds. He saw a rusty ladder that led up to a ledge on the tin roof. He wondered where exactly these guys were going to 'hang out', when he heard some boys chatting and laughing upstairs on the roof. Sahil took a deep breath and climbed onto the window. The moment he looked down, the pitch dark, never-ending black hole he saw made him giddy. He immediately turned his attention away, and focused on his steep climb. It didn't seem any less daunting when he wasn't looking down at the big black abyss that he could be in, if his balance gave way. He knew that very instant, there was no way students were officially allowed to be here. But not the one to give up on an adventure, Sahil climbed out the window. With one foot still dug into the window sill, he set the other on the ladder. As soon as he did this, a rusted piece of the paint on the ladder gave way, making a loud 'thud' sound almost 10 seconds later as it landed on the ground below. That was when Sahil realised that the height at which he was hanging off a ladder right now, was a way more dangerous situation than he had earlier thought he was in.

Sahil tried not to panic by thinking of the positive – the rest of the ladder was still intact, ensuring that he was still safe and sound. He focused on the rest of the climb up the ladder, carefully following every instruction Caesar had given him.

When he finally got to the roof, he was stunned by what he saw. The clear night sky studded with a blanket of bright, beautiful stars left him motionless. It was nothing like anything he had ever seen before, not even on any of the international trips that his parents had taken him for. He forgot all about where he was and was teleported to an alternate universe. And then, all of a sudden, he noticed one of the stars gliding leisurely across the sky. The moving star was moving at its own sweet pace and seemed so close, that for a moment he actually thought that if he puts his hand out he would actually be able to reach out and grab it. He had forgotten that he was still at Oakwood as he remained hypnotised like a child who had stepped into some fantasyland. Just then he heard the sound of Caesar's voice calling out to him. *"Bro! Don't be so stunned. It's not a UFO or anything. Just a satellite. You'll see a lot of them from up here since we are 8000 feet above sea level."*

For a brief moment, Sahil wanted to return to the enchanting world that he had been so abruptly hauled out of. But he looked around to see Caesar and his gang sitting at the ledge, and walked over to them. As he went closer, he noticed the boys passing around a beer bottle that one of them had managed to score on their last town visit. It had a cheap gold label on it that said 'Canon 10000'. Sahil noticed that the bottle looked very different from the sophisticated 30 year old scotch that his father stocked up in the bar at home. Caesar took a sip from the bottle and then passed it to Sahil, who just looked at it hesitantly. Picking up on the hesitation, Caesar threw the newcomer a rather surprised glance, *"Dude, don't tell me this is your first time!"*

Sahil reluctantly replied, *"Uhh… Yeah man, it is."*

Stunned by his latest discovery, Caesar started laughing uncontrollably, *"Haha, are you serious? Young child, get ready to step into adulthood."*

He pushed the bottle towards Sahil and almost forced him to take a big gulp of the beer. Sahil held his breath and went for a large glug, as if trying to prove that he wasn't any lesser of an adult than them. The bitter beer taste didn't go down too well with the novice.

He tossed the bottle over to Mann, "*There, happy? Now it's your turn!*"

The boys took turns enjoying the prized bottle, one after the other. A few sips later, the beer didn't feel all that bitter. In fact Sahil liked how unpleasant yet refreshing the beer tasted. The heady concoction of alcohol and the cool mountain breeze had given the first-timer more than a slight buzz. By the end of it, however, all of them were getting a little tipsy.

Caesar suddenly threw a trick question at Sahil, "*Dude, since this is you first time drinking, tell me, are you a virgin too?*"

Sahil trying his best to sound convincing, replied, "*Err virgin, me, err, no of course not...*" Caesar was even more shocked this time, than he was at the answer to the beer question. He jumped up and shrieked, "*Damn, you are a virgin!*"

He nudged Sahil who was visibly embarrassed by this very public announcement. All the other boys start laughing hysterically. Caesar hushed everyone down, as if about to make an important proclamation. Everyone immediately stopped, letting him continue his announcement, "*Well Mr. Madhavan, Maddy, roll number 423, it's your lucky day today. I'm going to take you straight to heaven!*"

Chapter 26

The boys jumped across the terrace, onto the other side of the dorm's wall. There was a dingy spiral staircase leading down to the front courtyard of the school. The entire gang carefully tiptoed across to the other side of campus, towards the girl's hostel. Caesar, who had led the way on this extremely dangerous operation, pulled an acrobatic stunt by climbing a pipe that led up to a window. He knocked on it, and looked around to see if anyone else was there.

Luckily, there was no one around except the boys themselves. They were right behind him, hanging off the pipe, with Sahil right at the end. Although extremely curious about where exactly they were going, Sahil asked no questions.

After a few minutes, there was a response to Caesar's knock. He could see a torchlight approaching the window. Someone discreetly opened the window and flashed the light down, blinding the boys for a few seconds. Caesar signalled them to follow him as he climbed into the window. Sahil who was the last one to enter an enclosed space of some kind, still wasn't sure where they were. As he looked around wondering, he saw more torchlights come on from various corners of the room. Beyond the lights he noticed the girls from school. It suddenly dawned upon him. *"Holy crap! We are in the girls' dorm?! Guys are we even supposed to be here?"*, he panicked as he whispered loudly. There was no response. When he looked around him, he saw none of the boys were there to answer his question. He was terrified as well as angry, as he was sure they had left him there in the arms of trouble before scooting away.

Just then, he noticed them in various corners of the room. They were all with their respective girlfriends, who looked more than happy chatting and giggling away with their boyfriends. The boys seemed to know the girls well, as it became obvious that most of them had girlfriends in that dorm. This sneaking around seemed to be a regular occurrence here, nothing out of the ordinary. As all the boys went on to spend quality time with their girlfriends, Sahil was left alone. As he looked around, he realised that the only girl around who didn't seem to have a boyfriend was Julie. The last time they had spoken was when she had stopped Sahil from making a fool of himself, by drilling sense into his head about Tina.

Both of them just sat there awkward, with nothing to say to each other. In an attempt to break the silence, Julie tried to mutter something. This only made it more awkward between them.

Julie, *"Err.. did you get your homework done?"*

Sahil just looked at her confused, not knowing how to respond to this bizarre question. Julie looked down at the floor, visibly embarrassed. Sahil smiled in his head at the fact that there was at least one more person in the world, as awkward as him around the opposite sex. Suddenly he felt a lot braver, and was about to attempt another conversation when he heard the loud whistling of a guard. The guard was trying to create commotion to raise an alarm, as he had seen several torchlights come on. He knew this meant that the boys had probably sneaked in. Sahil looked around, horrified. He didn't know what to do. Just then, Caesar and the gang came running to him and grabbed him, *"Dude, we've got to get out of here!"*

Caesar pulled Sahil along with him. As Sahil stumbled towards the window, he and Julie glanced back at each other. As they heard footsteps of the security guards and wardens running towards the dorm, Caesar, Sahil and the rest of the gang jumped out. They made a quiet, swift exit out of the girl's hostel, just about making it without getting caught. From the moment Sahil leapt out of the girl's dorm till he slipped under the blanket on his bed, it felt like he hadn't breathed at all. As soon as he lay still in bed, he realised that his heart was pounding out of his chest. He was pretty sure it was beating loud enough to wake up the entire dorm.

Luckily no one heard, neither did any of the wardens or security guards come looking for the troublemakers at the boys' dorms.

Chapter 27

The next morning after the assembly, Caesar was enthusiastically narrating the previous night's incident to Rudra, the head boy. The rest of the boys sniggered as they intently listened to him give a blow-by-blow account of the adventurous escape from the forbidden dorm.

"...And before I knew it, the bloody guard starts whistling. I pulled Sahil away from his new girlfriend and we jumped right out...", Caesar went on animatedly as he saw his audience lapping the story up. The excitement on the faces of those who weren't there to witness last night, encouraged Caesar to add his own harmless twists to his adventure-ridden tale. This amused Sahil, who was there listening all this while. But he let it pass. After all, Caesar had carried this entire operation out to help Sahil 'fix' his virginity issues.

Caesar's time in the spotlight was cut short abruptly by Mann, who came running towards them. The panic on his face immediately drew the attention of everyone who was gathered there in the courtyard. Caesar was slightly irritated by this unexpected shift of focus from him, but the news that Mann brought, soon made him forget all about it.

The exams were being preponed for all the batches, and the time they had was just not going to be enough to prepare for them. While the conversation was going on, Sahil suddenly remembered the ventilators in the staffroom. The last time he went there to pick some books up from Mrs. Pontford, he recalled noticing how these ventilators were permanently open. An extremely devilish idea started brewing in his mind. He mentally debated whether to make it public for a few seconds, before blurting it out.

Sahil looked around to make sure no one other than his batch mates were listening. He then started speaking, careful to maintain a hushed tone. *"I know how to get into the staffroom at night, undetected."* The boys' eyes widened the moment they heard this.

Sahil looked around once again before he continued, *"We could get a copy of the question papers and no one would know."*

"How?" Caesar asked. This time it was him on the audience side, lapping up each word that came out of Sahil's mouth.

Sahil took a long pause before he started revealing his master plan. *"Well, if we found a way to keep the security busy, someone could climb in through the ventilators, get the papers and climb back out. The staffroom remains locked from the outside and nobody would ever know what's going on inside."*

Caesar interrupted him, *"And you think it's that easy? Who's going to take the risk of climbing in?"*

Without giving a thought to the consequences, Sahil promptly volunteered. *"I will. I'm quite sure I'll fit through. I just need help from everyone else to do their bit to keep me off the grid and we'll be fine."*

"No way dude, its way too risky", Caesar dismissed the idea.

Sahil debated, *"Exactly, that's why nobody would even guess it has happened! It's perfect. Besides, we could even sell the papers to students you trust. Think about it! After all, what choice do we have?"*

All Caesar could think of was the various possibilities of this operation failing, and Sahil getting himself into some serious danger, *"Dude, this is insane!"*

As the two argued, the other boys tried to debate the plan in their own minds too. Was it worth it? Would they get caught? What if they got caught? Everyone was waiting for someone else to give his opinion on the matter.

Just then, Rudra who had been listening to them intently, interrupted. Everyone was curious about what his viewpoint was going to be, as he began to speak. *"Sahil's right. We don't really have any choice here. We're screwed if we don't have the papers! Sahil, will you take on this responsibility and organise the operation?"*

Sahil, who was eager to please his new friends and prove himself to be worthy of their company wasn't going to back down at this point. He was ready to take the risk and jumped at the opportunity to plan the entire operation.

Sahil assured Rudra, *"Absolutely Rudra. Trust me, I'm going to get the papers out."* Rudra and the rest of the boys didn't know Sahil well enough. But whatever little they knew was enough to prove that he meant business. However, they still weren't sure if he would be able to carry such a major heist on his shoulders or not. Caesar stepped towards Sahil, as if to show his support and willingness to participate in the plan. "Alright then, this is your gig… What's the plan?"

Proud of this sudden position of command that he was in, Sahil immediately got to work. He remembered one of the stories that his grandfather would tell him from his army days, during his time as the Commanding Officer at the front, in the Bangladesh War. He had planned and executed an entire high-risk operation, capturing an important enemy stronghold post. Each time Sahil listened to the story that his grandfather often told him during bedtime, the little boy would imagine himself in his place, heading a military squad on a mission. The same feeling returned after years. And just like his grandpa, Sahil too dived full-throttle into this different kind of 'mission' that he had taken up.

Chapter 28

That day Sahil was restless through class. Planning a strategy for a top-secret operation wasn't easy after all. In the afternoon history class, he started scribbling the layout of the school on a piece of paper. After mentally working out the task he was assigned with, he couldn't wait to share it with Caesar and the others. He passed on a message to the guy on the next seat, *"4.30 pm, dorm"*, and signalled him to pass it on to the rest of the guys. By the end of history class, all the boys knew the time and venue of their meet-up after school.

As soon as the bell for the last class rang, the boys jumped out of their seats and were on their way to the dorm. Everyone was excited to be a part of the plan, and no one wanted to be left out.

Back at the dorm, Sahil, Caesar, Jatin and a bunch of other students were all peering over the tattered piece of paper in which Sahil had drawn up the plan. He started explaining his strategy step-by-step to his batch mates, *"Ok guys, here's the plan. We will strike this Friday night, two hours after lights out at sharp 12:00 am. It's the beginning of the weekend and most teachers wouldn't bother making a surprise visit to the dorms. The seniors will be sleeping by this time so they won't be a problem."*

The leader in him took over and soon he was assigning duties to the boys. He pointed to Jatin as he continued, *"Sethi, the security guards are Sikhs. So your main task with Mann is that you have to go and talk to them in Punjabi, distract them, give them a quarter of rum, talk about Punjab... Do whatever it takes to keep them distracted cause if you fail, we are busted!"*

The more he spoke, the more confident he felt about himself and his plan. It wasn't just about getting through the exam for Sahil. It was a lot more than that. There are two kinds of people in this world – ones that settle for being the crowd, and the others that don't settle for any lesser than being crowd-pullers. Though completely unaware, Sahil belonged to the second kind. He enjoyed being in control, and watching everyone eat out of his palms that evening felt good.

Within a matter of weeks, the meek, awkward teenager had turned into a leader the entire batch was turning to for solutions.

Those who started out as his enemies had turned into his cronies. And his friends had become his loyalists.

Sahil was focused as he continued explaining the operation, " *Ankit and Rahul, I want you two stationed in your night suits on the north end of the dorms. Keep a watch for seniors who might be awake and around. If you see anyone, you will flash your torch thrice to the south end. Then you will go to the bathrooms, pretending to use the toilet.*"

He then moved on to instruct everyone from the batch systematically, "Varun and Ashish, you two will be at the south end and if you see them flash their torches, you'll flash your torches to Namit and Anurag who will be our eyes and ears near the staff room. If you two see their torches you two have to run to us and tell us. The operation will be terminated."

The boys spent the next 3 days, going over the plan multiple times. The piece of paper on which Sahil had detailed out the entire mission, became somewhat of a bible for the batch. He would keep it hidden right under his bed, and anyone who had any doubt with about the plan, knew where to find the answers. It had specific instructions for each team of two boys that were going to be stationed at different points. These teams that Sahil referred to as 'units', would physically go through the mission multiple times every night after lights out. It was the last night before D-Day. The end of the 3-day boot camp was marked by a talk by Sahil, *"Guys we all know our roles, our part in the mission. Without even one of us, the entire mission is going to fail. So I want you all to focus 100% of your energy into tomorrow night. We've got this!"*

That Saturday night, none of the boys slept at lights out. Precisely 1 hour and 55 minutes after lights out, each one jumped out of bed and walked to their respective positions. Save the night vision goggles, masks and weapons, this looked like a full-fledged commando mission. Each unit was moving so swift and smooth, that unless one had super human hearing, their footsteps were next to inaudible. They attained positions at the exact points that they were instructed to.

Sethi and Mann went over to the watchmen and began chatting with them in broken Punjabi-Hindi. "Hore paaji kiddan? Sab wadiya? Aj mainu apne ghar di bhoth yaad aa rahi hai , maa di haath di paki rotiya di yaad aa rahi hai. Mera parivar naal beh ke roti khane da ji kar raya hai, teh sab toh wadh ke apne Punjab di yaad aa rahi hai (How are you bro? All well? Today I am missing home... Missing the food, my family.. Missing my Punjab)" The Punjab connection had served as more than just an icebreaker between the boys and the watchman. It had the unsuspecting chachaji completely engrossed in conversation, reminiscing about Punjab with the two.

Ankit and Rahul stood in attention at the north end, while Varun and Ashish assumed their positions at the south end. Namit and Anurag guarded the staff room. Each unit kept a 360-degree watch, making sure they didn't have any company while Caesar, Kumar and Karan helped Sahil break into the staff room.

The four of them were to make a human pyramid, as per the plan. And Sahil, who was the leanest of them all, would climb over them with a rope. His next move would be to go through the ventilator, get the papers, Xerox them, and then climb back up to the ventilator using the rope. All of this had to happen in exactly TEN MINUTES. Within ten minutes, the entire operation had to be carried out. That's when the first unit, Jatin and Mann would head back to the dorm, followed by the other units.

After a while, Jatin and Mann had run out of conversation with the watchmen. Jatin was beginning to get anxious. Sahil climbed down the rope, inside the staff room. If there was one observation he had made during his regular visits to the staff room, it was that the Vice Principal always kept the most important documents, right from exam papers to report cards. The Principal was too busy for operational duties, and hence, would assign the important ones to the second in command. Without wasting any time, he went straight to the Vice Principal's desk.

Sahil frantically looked for the papers in the desk, but couldn't find them. Sethi looked at his watch. It had been 9 minutes and 45 seconds since the operation had begun. Time was nearly up, and he was now anxious to know if Sahil and the rest had been successful or if they had been busted. Even Caesar, Kumar and Karan were getting impatient. With 15 seconds to go, Sahil still wasn't out of that staff room. Just when the boys right outside the staffroom started getting impatient, Sahil climbed out of the ventilator, untied the rope and jumped down. Noticing that Sahil had no papers in his hand, Caesar and the rest were disappointed. However, before anyone could say anything, their watch alarms started beeping. Now the second leg of the mission had started – making sure no one gets busted. They all discreetly ran off to the dorms. Jatin, whose watch had started beeping too, gestured Mann that they had to leave. Mann let out a yawn, as if sleepy and said his goodbye to the watchman, and both of them made a smooth exit. All the watch units ran to their dorms as well. They got into their respective beds quietly, as if they had been there the whole time. The boys were all glad to finally be back in their dorm without getting busted. As the adrenalin started wearing off, they realised that they still didn't have any papers.

Caesar whispered in the dark, loud enough for Sahil and the rest of the boys to hear. "*Shit man, you didn't find it? I knew this wasn't going to work. Thank God we didn't get busted!*"

Sahil, grinning wide in the dark, "*I never said I didn't get it buddy.*"

He pulled out a bundle of folded papers from his pocket, and flashed his torchlight on them for Caesar and everyone else to see!

Chapter 29

The boys couldn't believe what they had just heard. They were suddenly all wide-awake now. Still gleaming from the victory, Sahil got out of bed and headed to the bathroom. On the way, he signalled Caesar to come with him. Sahil took a deep breath before handing over the crumpled but valuable bundle of papers to Rudra, who was waiting for them in the bathroom. He still couldn't believe that these boys had executed such a high-risk heist.

Rudra admitted, "*I'll be damned.. I never thought you'll would pull it off!*"

Sahil was grinning with pride. He had won a lot of medals and awards at his previous school in sports like swimming, basketball and cricket too. But none of those achievements had felt this good. This time, although he didn't win any medals, winning his batch mates' trust and confidence made him feel more powerful than ever before.

Caesar looked on proudly too as he added in, "*Well I always believed in him, after all he's my discovery.*"

Rudra elbowed him teasingly, "*Yeah, whatever, I saw how freaked out you were the last couple days!*"

Rudra looked at Sahil with newfound respect, as he spoke, "*You've got guts, my friend. And brains. It's a rare combination. I see big things ahead for you.*" He patted Sahil on the back and handed him a 1000 rupees, "*Here, this is for you all. Go enjoy yourselves.*" Sahil was pleasantly surprised. The unexpected reward was the icing on the cake.

Rudra turned back to Caesar with instructions, "*Caesar, quietly start pushing the papers out, but only to students you 100% trust. Sell it at 100 bucks a piece. Now go bloody enjoy!*"

Chapter 30

Sahil became an overnight sensation, quite literally. Over the next few days, the story of his heroic feat spread across the rest of the batch as well. Caesar and his gang got busy with the trade of test papers in the coming week. The entire batch had bought them out at the Rs.100 price.

Next Sunday, the students had their monthly town leave. Sahil and the boys decided to head to the cosy town of Nainital to celebrate with their 'hard earned' money. This was the first time Sahil was stepping out of school premises since he had arrived here. As they walked out to the gates, he silently relived the time that he had gotten off that bus and walked through the lonely trails that welcomed him at Oakwood. It seemed like so long ago – not as much in terms of time, as the person he had become. He could no more relate to the meek boy who had walked into Oakwood a couple of months earlier. Sahil saw his friends a few feet ahead of him and he scampered ahead to catch up with them. And just as he ran, in those few seconds, he had left behind whatever little was left of the unsure 14 year old that walked up these roads a few weeks back.

After almost a three-kilometre walk downhill, they were in the small yet picturesque town of Nainital. The last time Sahil was in this town, he had arrived from Bombay with his bags and baggage – both physical and emotional. The gloomy little village that he remembered it to be had made way for a brighter, sunnier one. He realised at that moment that it had more to do with his state-of-mind than the actual look of the town.

At the town centre, a group of girls from school were already standing there. They were waiting for the boys to come, after which they would spend the day around town with them. Sahil was pleasantly surprised to see Julie there too. With her eyes crinkled under the sun, she flashed a warm smile at Sahil. He smiled back. Before he could say anything else, the rest of the boys had already decided that they would be treating the girls to a film and lunch. They all headed off to the only cinema hall in Nainital town, Capitol.

Once they arrived, Sahil noticed the movie poster and realised that there was a C-grade film playing. He glanced across at Julie who seemed slightly uncomfortable, as she stared at the poster.

Sahil noticed this, and suggested that the two of them skip the film and meet the rest for lunch later. Julie looked visibly relieved with the change of plan. Caesar winked and gave him a thumbs-up.

The two stepped out of the theatre and walked down the cobbled street. Julie finally spoke for the first time since the two had met here in town.
She blushed, *"Thanks for backing out of the movie because of me."*
Sahil was pleased with himself but replied matter-of-factly, *"It was nothing."*

They headed towards a fun-n-fair, a few blocks down. As they arrived at the entrance, they saw brightly lit up rides; vendors selling ram ladoos (a tamarind based local sweet) and sour treats; game stalls and beyond it all a multi-coloured giant ferris wheel.

Julie's eyes lit up like a 5 year old at the sight of the giant wheel. Excited, she asked Sahil if he would like to go on it. Before he could answer, she had already made a queue for the ride. Soon, it was their turn to get in. The operator directed them towards the yellow cart right in the front, and secured the lock as soon as they got in. Now that they were locked in, the cart seemed a lot smaller than it looked. The sudden awareness of proximity between the two was interrupted by the jumpstarting of the giant wheel. For the first few seconds, Julie enjoyed the butterflies in the tummy. But within no time, the wheel was going a lot faster than she had anticipated. Scared, she reached out to Sahil's hand next to hers and held it tight. Now he had butterflies in his tummy too, and the giant wheel ride had nothing to do with it. Just when Julie was about to settle down from the initial fear, their cart reached right at the top and stayed suspended there. She panicked and without thinking, hid her face in Sahil's chest. Astonished and unable to move, Sahil just held still. He was sure she could hear his heart that was now beating faster than the engine of an F1 car.

When the ride came to an end, neither of them realised it. The man working the wheel unlocked their car and announced for them to get off. As she slowly opened her eyes, she noticed Sahil looking closely at her. Something had changed between them. Suddenly, both were aware of some unexplained feelings.

Clueless about what it was, the only thing they knew was that there was no other place they'd rather be than in this big scary giant wheel. They stared at each other for what seemed like an eternity, till the operator shook their cart impatiently, asking them to get off again.

Chapter 31

Sahil got off the giant wheel first, and then helped Julie climb down. He kept holding on to her hand even after she had gotten off. She didn't seem to mind it. The two walked away hand in hand. Out of all the girls he had met so far at Oakwood, she was the most innocent and child-like. Her waif-like body made her look so vulnerable; he couldn't help but feel like he had to protect her. And yet, she had a calming, almost motherly effect on him. They hadn't known each other for too long. But she had been the only one who could put sense into his head, when nothing or no one else made sense.

As they started walking out of the fun-n-fair, Julie spotted a cotton candy vendor. She ran towards the vendor, once again dragging Sahil along. He gave the vendor an extra five rupees, signalling him to make it a supersized blob of cotton candy. The smile on Julie's face, on seeing her extra large cotton candy ball, was one Sahil couldn't erase off his mind for a long time after that day.

Once they headed out of the fair, the playful mood made way for a quieter, romantic day. The two walked around town hand in hand, enjoying the scenic city as much as each other's company. Sahil checked his calculator watch that had started beeping. Unfortunately, it was time to head towards the theatre to catch up with their friends again. They all ate lunch together. The two spent the rest of the afternoon stealing glances and holding hands when no one was watching. The rest of the group decided to head back to school early, while Julie suggested that they go ahead as she wanted to show Sahil around town a little bit longer. They spent a beautiful rest of the day together.

As Sahil and Julie walked back to school later that evening, neither of them said a word to each other. They strolled with their hands clasped tight, both secretly wishing for time to pause at that moment. The two of them were half way to school when Sahil noticed something glistening under the faint moonlight, on the unevenly cobbled pathway. It was a four-leaf clover. Thrilled to have found something so rare, he immediately picked it up and gave it to Julie. She took it and looked at him fondly. There was something different about the way she was looking at his face, studying every part of it. She then blushed as she put her arms around him, before leaning forward to give him a lingering kiss on his lips. That day on, they both believed that the clover had in some mystical way, given their relationship a pure new beginning.

Originally, the four-leaf clover is a rare variation of the common three-leaf clover. According to tradition, these sprigs bring good luck to their finders, especially if found accidentally. In fact it is so rare that there are 10,000 three-leaf ones for every four-leaf one. Each leaf is believed to represent something significant – the first is for faith, the second is for hope, the third represents love and the fourth is for luck.

Sahil and Julie started getting closer with each passing day. They studied together; she was there to cheer him on at every single basketball match (including practice matches). The two even spent the weekends together, just walking around town. When Sahil wasn't busy making money through the stealing and peddling of papers with his gang, he was spending time with Julie. She was the only 'normal' in his otherwise eventful life. The two were falling madly in love with each other. They would spend time sitting at the broken end of the courtyard wall, overlooking the charming town of Nainital. One evening, he opened up to her about his life before Oakwood. He spoke and spoke, and then he suddenly stopped. He looked at her to realise that she was looking at him smiling, connected to his soul. Without thinking, he leant towards her and kissed her.

He bared every little truth, fear and weakness that he had survived in his 14-year-old life. She knew everything about him, except his dual life here at Oakwood. Sahil would shower her with gifts that he bought from the money he made from his very profitable 'exam paper business'. Julie was completely unaware of this side of Sahil's life, and he intended to keep it that way. He didn't want his alternate life to spoil what he had with Julie, and vice versa.

One evening, when both of them were sitting at the courtyard wall, watching the sunset, Sethi came running towards Sahil. Panting and huffing, he finally managed to speak, *"Sahil, bro, hurry up! The principal has called us all in, at the dorm."*

Chapter 32

Sahil looked at Julie, who seemed puzzled by this unusual call for assembly by the Principal. Without saying a word to her, he ran with Jatin to the dorms. On the way, he thought of at least fifteen different reasons as to why the principal had to talk to them so urgently. As they reached the entrance, Sahil and Jatin saw the entire batch standing in a straight line with their heads down. The two walked to the farthest end of the line and joined it. Mr. Pontford was yet to arrive.

None of the boys dared to look anywhere else but the floor. After a few minutes, they could all hear Mr. Pontford's angry footsteps pacing towards to their dorm. The principal stormed into the dorm, ignoring the tentative *'Good Evening Sir'* that the boys muttered. For the first time, his spectacles were off, and his calm and composed demeanour had made way for an intimidating man who was capable of stirring up a storm. His eyes, wide with rage, sized up every single boy carefully as he paced down the dorm room. Mr. Pontford finally spoke. The first few words struck the entire batch like lightning. His voice thundered, *"You all have dared to break into the staff room and leak the papers out. Never before has this school had to deal with such disgraceful crooks. This batch is a black mark on the history of Oakwood."* He asked the culprits to own up, but not even a single person uttered a word.

"I give you exactly 30 seconds to come forward if you have done it, or tell me who did it." Everyone stayed mum and so he suspended the entire batch instructing them not to leave their dorms for the next week. Before the shocked students could say anything, he had already stormed out just as fast as he had stormed in.

Even after he left, the boys stood there in disbelief. Someone had ratted them out!

Chapter 33

The boys spent the day trying to put a finger on who must have gone rogue on them. That evening, as the rest of the batches returned to their dorms, one of the juniors, Rahul, came up to Caesar. He was usually the first one to get in on valuable information at Oakwood. No one knew how he did it, but they trusted him. After all, so far his information had been accurate 100% of the times.

The junior spoke in a hurried manner, as he wanted to finish off and get back to his dorm without being spotted by anyone else. *"Bro! I saw Rana talking to the principal yesterday. In fact, I'm hundred percent sure I heard him saying that Sahil was the mastermind behind the break in. And that the whole batch was involved."*

Sahil was red with rage when he heard this. He clenched his teeth tight, trying to hold his anger back. Just then, Rana walked into the dorm. He chuckled as he saw the entire batch sitting quietly. Everyone ignored him. He continued smirking as he spoke, *"How sad… Now Sahil won't be able to meet Julie for a whole week! Maybe she too will dump him and start seeing me. Don't worry Sahil, I'll take good care of her."* He grinned from cheek to cheek as he finished his last sentence.

Sahil lost complete control of his temper and threw a hard punch at Rana. The two went after each other like two warring bison. Suddenly, Rana's friends jumped into the fight, and so did Caesar, Sethi, Mann and the rest of Sahil's batch mates. There was complete chaos in the dorm room till Rudra intervened. The head boy in him took over and the authority in his voice suddenly sounded intimidating as he yelled at everyone to stop fighting immediately.

Once everyone stopped to pay attention to him, he spoke in a calm but firm manner. *"Gentlemen, we are Oakwoodians and not street thugs to get in gang wars. If you'll want to settle this, I suggest you do it as men, in the ring!"*

The boys agreed, and immediately, beds were dragged together to form a makeshift ring in the dorm.

Chapter 34

The two got into the 'ring', like gladiators did in the arena. Their respective batch mates were cheering each on. The entire dorm was clearly divided into Rana's supporters and Sahil's supporters. By now, the word had spread in the rest of the dorms too about the fight. More spectators from the junior as well as senior batches had gathered around. No one wanted to miss the part-2 of an epic scene that had taken place at the beginning of school year, when Rana had beaten Sahil to pulp. Since then, a lot had changed. Except that the two had never looked eye-to-eye again. Everyone knew about how Tina had played Sahil, just to get back with Rana. And whoever knew this, also knew that the equation between Sahil and Rana was a ticking time bomb, waiting to explode.

Rudra blew the whistle like in a real fight, and the two started boxing. Everything about this fight looked professional – the setting, the crowd cheering, the ring. Only, neither of them had gloves or mouth guards on. The cheers got louder, with everyone chanting either Rana's name or Sahil's.

Rana was the bigger, beefier one out of the two. His thug-like frame worked to his advantage, as he threw punch after punch at Sahil's face. Blood instantly started trickling down his white uniform shirt, and within no time it had turned completely bloody. After a few blows, Sahil's vision started getting foggy. Every time he went to punch Rana, he would miss. He fell to the ground multiple times, each time picking himself up instantly. The cheering grew fainter and fainter, with every fall. Everyone watching started getting concerned for Sahil. He could hear the crowd from both sides, screaming at him to stay down. However, every time he heard that, it persuaded him to get back up.

Midway through the fight, Rana swung a full-on punch across Sahil's face. The skinny 14 year old fell straight to the ground, face first. Blood started trickling down his nose and a stinging sensation caused his eyes to tear up. The crowd suddenly went silent and watched in horror, as the youngster lost all control of his body and lay still. The only visible movement was of the blood streaming out of his nose and onto the floor. Everyone stood still, watching, as it continued to trickle rapidly through the crevices of the wood flooring.

Sahil could faintly hear someone giving the countdown in the background. *2,3,4...* He had no energy left to take on any more punches and was ready to give up. Just then, Rana walked up to him and spat on his face, uttering the word "BASTARD" as he started walking away. The word speared through Sahil's head and gushed through his veins like newfound adrenaline. His body twitched, as suddenly his brain was flooded with images of both his parents.

The count had reached 6. Suddenly, in a matter of milliseconds, Sahil had regained all his senses. He was up on his feet, now completely unaware of the blood or the pain. Rana went ahead to punch him again, and right then something took over Sahil. He attacked Rana with an animalistic force, throwing blow after blow at him. The big built prefect, who was about to fall to the floor, crouched helplessly like an infant. His face was now covered in blood, but Sahil who kept pounding it, showed no sign of stopping. The senior looked like he was about to faint at any moment, but Sahil held him up and kept punching him ruthlessly. Watching this magical turn of events, the entire crowd started cheering for Sahil, including Rana's friends. After all, they all knew what a merciless beast Rana was. Watching him suffer like he had made many others suffer, gave them all some kind of secret pleasure.

Sahil finally let go of Rana. He fell to the ground, knocked out. This time, Sahil spat on him before walking around the crowd as they cheered even louder. He started screaming his own name, getting high on the adulation as if it were a drug. Sahil had discovered a beast within himself that he never knew existed.

With this fight, something in him had changed, and so had how everyone else looked at him. That night, all everyone was talking about was this menacing new version of Sahil's personality that the fight had unearthed.

Chapter 35

Next morning, the suspended batch was hanging around at the dorm. None of them were really treating the suspension as anything more than a mini vacation, right inside school. Some were practicing football while others were still reliving last night's fight. If the staffroom feat had won Sahil some kind of heroic status, the fight with Rana had sealed it.

Sahil's face and body were bruised, but not defeated. He sat on his bed with an icepack in one hand, nursing his swollen lip that had ripped. In the other hand he was holding a piece of paper, reading it intently. The calm on his face was a complete turnaround from the animal that had taken over the previous night.

The piece of paper that he was so engrossed in, was a letter from his father. As he read it carefully, his dad's austere voice began playing in his head, "*I hope you are well son. It's always heart warming to read your letters and learn about how much progress you have made at school. You know, it wasn't an easy decision for me to send you away, but I now feel that it was the right one. I spoke to Mrs. Pontford a few weeks back and she tells me that you are one of the top students in the class. I am very proud of you son. Keep it up.*"

By the time Sahil had finished reading the letter, his father's tone had changed into a softer, gentler one. Through that one piece of paper, the 14 year old felt the warmth that he had been longing for. Sahil's eyes glistened as a tear welled up. He knew that his father would be very disappointed with him had he known what Sahil was really up to. After all, this was one of the few times he had felt a glimmer of pride for him, in his father.

Suddenly, out of nowhere, a football came and hit the teenager. Caesar had kicked it towards him, "*Dude, stop being a sissy. Come play with us.*" Sahil quickly gulped, as if to swallow the lump that had formed in his throat. He switched to his cool, playful demeanour as he picked the ball and threw it towards Caesar.

Just then, a junior came running into the dorm, and informed Sahil that Mrs. Pontford had called for him immediately.

Chapter 36

In the staffroom, there were a few labourers walking in and out. Sahil straightened his shirt, made sure his hair was in place, and cleared his throat before he stepped in. He noticed the labourers fitting bars on the ventilators and windows of the entire staffroom, protecting it from any further break-ins. A slight smile ran across his face, before he made it disappear as quickly as he could. He was suddenly aware that he had to be careful not to drop even a hint about the secret mission that he and the boys had carried out.

He noticed Mrs. Pontford sitting in her cabin, trying hard to focus on getting some workbooks corrected. She looked slightly distracted. Sahil knocked on the door and tried to study the elegant 60 year old's expressions through her rimless glasses. She seemed concerned, as she looked up at Sahil. She smiled faintly before inviting him to sit next to her.

Mrs. Pontford held Sahil's hand as she spoke, *"Son, the word is that it was you who orchestrated the whole break-in. I fail to believe so. I know you probably are being blamed for something you haven't done. But I just need to hear it from you."*

She looked down at the floor as if deciding the best way to ask the next question. *"Son, tell me the truth, did all this have anything to do with you?"*

The worried look on her face made it seem like there was only one answer she really wanted to hear. And he wasn't about to disappoint her. After giving it a split second's thought, he replied, *"No ma'am I, didn't even know any of this was happening. Whoever has done it, obviously didn't even trust me."*

Mrs. Pontford looked relieved as she continued speaking in her soft, composed tone, *"I knew it. Son, now listen to me carefully. I know you have been hanging around Caesar and his group. I suspect they were the ones behind this and everyone thinks it's you. Stay away from them. You are an ace student and a good boy and their company will only spoil you. You understand me?"*

Sahil replied, *"Yes ma'am."*

Mrs. Pontford was now smiling, *"Good, now go back to your dorm before my husband sees you."*

Sahil walked out of the staffroom, and heaved a sigh of relief. However, suddenly a sick feeling in the pit of his tummy overcame him. Relief had quickly made way for guilt, as something dawned upon him.

It had been so easy for him to lie to Mrs. Pontford, the one person he respected immensely. She was the first person who had given him the confidence and courage to have a voice when he had walked into Oakwood. She had trusted him more than anyone else ever had in his entire life.

He knew he had changed. But was the change so drastic, that even he couldn't recognise the person he had turned into? Had the popularity blinded him so much that he couldn't tell the difference between right and wrong anymore?

He dismissed his thoughts right before entering the dorm, and put his usual care-a-damn face on.

Chapter 37

Later that evening, Mr. Pontford was pacing around in his home. It was a beautiful Victorian villa at the far end of the school's courtyard. The white window panes with beautiful lattice work curtains; the wooden flooring that creaked every time one walked around the house; the vintage furniture upholstery that matched perfectly with the rest of the interiors and the fireplace; all of it gave the villa a warm countryside feel. One could see that the home had been meticulously taken care of with utmost pride, by the woman of the house.

Mr. Pontford lit his pipe as he stood there, thoughtfully looking out of the window. *"No I know he was definitely involved, I can't let him off suspension."*

The worried expression was back on Mrs. Pontford's face as she defended Sahil. *"And I know he wasn't involved. Your information is incorrect. I know this boy, he is a sincere kid."*

The two had been having a heated argument about Sahil's involvement in the staffroom break-in episode for a few days now. Both of them were of two opposite opinions. Mrs. Pontford's judgement was obviously fogged by the soft corner she had for the boy.

Mr. Pontford was firm about what he believed in, *"You have misjudged him. He is a crook and mark my words, he will always be one. As far as his suspension is concerned, the whole batch is suspended and I won't change that. That's final."*

Mr. Pontford, too, had begun to grow fond of the bright youngster. But years of experience handling batches of boys, he knew better than to get blinded by notions. He had seen Sahil veer towards company like Caesar and his gang. He had also noticed the drastic change in his personality from being a sincere and meticulous student to a bold and boisterous teenager. And his gut told him that Sahil had been more than a mere spectator in the entire exam paper fiasco.

Chapter 38

A few days had passed by since the suspension was announced. The classroom looked half empty with only the girls in it. The boys however, were enjoying themselves, blissfully ignorant of the fact that they had been punished. The only thing they missed about class was seeing their girlfriends.

However, if boarding school had taught these Oakwoodians one thing, it was resilience. Whether it was the most inconsequential feats or the biggest missions, they all believed that where there was a will there was a way. And with this belief, the suspended boys devised a plan to catch up with their girlfriends.

One afternoon, after the sharp school bell rang announcing lunch break, Julie and her friends hurriedly left the classroom. They marched quickly to a back courtyard where anyone hardly ever went. This courtyard was right below the first floor boys' dorm bathrooms. Back in one of the shower cubicles the boys had created a makeshift phone booth, brilliantly engineered with some cups and strings. The bathroom stall had a small vent right on top that opened into the back courtyard where the girls were waiting. The boys lowered one end of the cup and string apparatus through the window, and kept the other end on their own side of the cubicle. Caesar's girlfriend, Rhea was the first one to grab the cup, as she tried to talk to him. Barely had she said a 'hi' when another girl snatched it and tried talking to Mann. Even back in the bathroom cubicle, it was utter chaos with every boy trying to get his two minutes of romantic rendezvous with his girlfriend.

Just as Mann was still mustering the courage to utter an 'I love you' to his girlfriend Seema, Sahil stepped in and took the cup from him. As he tried to speak to Julie, Sahil looked around to see the rest of the boys shamelessly listening to his conversation. He playfully snapped, "*Guys, I need to talk to Julie. Some privacy please!*"

The other boys feigned disappointment on hearing this, but headed off outside the bathroom stall, giving him his privacy. The girls too started walking off, since most of them were done talking to their boyfriends/crushes, leaving Julie alone.

This was the longest the two had gone without speaking to each other since the day they had gotten onto that giant wheel. Julie could sense the excitement in Sahil's voice as he spoke, "*How're you babe?*"

She smiled as she replied, "*Good baby, but I miss you.*"

He looked behind and saw that one of the boys was eavesdropping. Sahil shooed him away as he spoke, "*I miss you too.*"

Julie's voice sounded like a little girl as she complained, "*But I miss you more.*"

"*No I do.*"

"*Ok maybe you do then*", she giggled.

"*Haha. So what's happening out there?*"

Julie filled him in on the situation, "*Not much, its weird to be in a half empty class with only girls for the last couple of days.*"

Sahil assured her, "*Don't worry babe, it's only a couple of days more.*"

"*Hmm! By the way, guess what? You have become a big star at school.*"

"What do you mean?"

"*Well, firstly you'll managed to not get caught breaking into the staffroom for so many weeks. Then you beat up Rana. The whole school knows about it and you are their new hero!*"

Sahil, feeling flattered, "*Haha, yeah right!*"

"*No really, trust me!*"

Just then, the sharp school bell rang in the background, interrupting their conversation. Julie looked around, realising only then that the rest of the girls had left, "*I better get going for lunch honey.*"

"Ok, but give me a kiss."

"Here, how?" Julie smiled as she shyly played with her hair as if Sahil was right in front of her, watching her.

"Over the phone. That'll be good for now, later you can give me one in person."

Sahil's witty replies always made her blush. She coyly sneaked in a 'tele-kiss', *"Haha, ok, muaaah."*

"Muah back. See you soon baby."

Chapter 39

The next day, the boys were still in bed at 5.30 am when Mr. Pontford walked into the dorm and yelled "EVERYONE WAKE UP!" at the top of his high baritone voice. Startled, each and every one of them jumped out and stood in attention by their beds.

The cold autumn air was blowing through windows as well as the door behind Mr. Pontford, creating a chill around the dorm room. The orange-yellow sun that had just about risen made for a postcard moment as it peeked through the mountains.

Mr. Pontford paced around the dorm in his usual manner as he spoke, "*So, it's been 6 days into your suspension, and I have decided to reduce a day of it. I hope you all have learnt a valuable lesson.*"

"*Yeah, football!*" Caesar murmured to himself. On hearing this, the other boys around chuckled discreetly, trying hard to hold back their laughter.

"*I want you'll to get up and join the rest of the school for breakfast and resume classes.*" Mr. Pontford announced and walked over to Sahil.

He stared at Sahil just for a few seconds. But that was enough to make him nervous.

He weighed each word as he spoke, "*My wife thinks you were innocent, but I know you are a bad apple. I just hope you prove me right. Dismissed.*"

Saying this, he walked out. The boys started dancing around the dorm, giving each other high fives. They were celebrating the fact that they had gone scot-free for the exam paper heist, with a mini-vacation as a punishment.

Only Sahil stood there still. His guilt had suddenly multiplied after hearing Mr. Pontford's words. If there was one thing Sahil had never intentionally done in his life, it was lying. Being an army officer's son, honesty was a policy that was never taken lightly in his household. His father's face and the thought that he would be so disappointed if he ever found out what Sahil had been up to at Oakwood kept haunting him.

Caesar came running to him with his towel, and pushed him to the bathroom, *"Hurry up! You don't want to be late for the first day of school after being crowned SUPERSTAR!"* This was enough to get the 14-year-old Sahil distracted.

Chapter 40

The boys walked into the dining hall in a pack. Most of the school was already there, assembled for breakfast. As they walked in, every student looked at them with pride and respect in their eyes. They looked less like a class that had just been ordered out of suspension, and more like soldiers returning home from war.

As the boys entered, walking one after the other in a row, one of the juniors broke into impromptu claps. The rest of the students, all followed suit one after the other. Within seconds, the entire dining hall had erupted into a sea of claps and thumps on the dining tables.

As Sahil entered, the claps got louder and louder, finally reaching a deafening crescendo. Sahil, who had never faced such adulation before was soaking in every bit of glory that the crowd was showering him with. The quiet child, who preferred to get lost in the background till a few months back, had suddenly found himself on the centre stage enjoying demi-God like status. And instead of shying away from this limelight, Sahil enjoyed it more than anything else in the world.

While looking around at the crowd that was still cheering and clapping for them, he noticed Tina clapping too. And right next to her was Rana, who was the only one that looked enraged. Sahil surprised himself with the cruel pleasure he got out of this. But he didn't mind it, and definitely wasn't feeling guilty about it.

He breathed a deep, satisfying breath as he took it all in. This, so far, had been the single high point of his life ever. And he wanted to experience every little tingle of that high he was going through in those few moments.

Chapter 41

Sahil's popularity continued to grow over the next few months. The batch was now one big united gang led by the 14 year old. Whether it was brokering peace between a guy and his girlfriend or between two warring batch mates, he was the one everyone went to. Any problems that the juniors faced, even with prefects, they sought his intervention. He took great pride and pleasure in being the one guy everyone turned to for help. In fact, Sahil's rising fame spread beyond Oakwood. Even the rival school students started recognising him. If there was any friction between them and the Oakwoodians, Sahil and his gang were prompt to jump in and take them on in fights.

Down in the town of Nainital, small restaurant owners and shopkeepers on Mall Road had seen Sahil and his group take on fights with much bigger guys than themselves. And the fact that the frontman of this gang was a regular teenager, probably smaller than most of the guys he fought, turned him into some kind of a hero amongst them. Every weekend when he would come to town with his friends or with Julie, they would offer him complimentary soft drinks, bun omelettes and ice-creams.

Sahil's nature was turning more and more competitive with each passing day. Even in sports, his previously friendly personality had made way for an aggressive sportsman who refused to lose a single win. Once while playing a game of football, the defender from the opponent team deliberately kicked Sahil in his shin, causing a painful injury. The studded shoes instantly cut through his skin, causing blood to ooze out through his socks. Sahil was asked to rest for the remaining part of the game. However, at half-time, he spoke to the coach and insisted that he was fine and argued that he should really be back in the game. The coach finally gave in. Then, when the ball was passed to Sahil next, the same defender who had injured him came forward to tackle him again. Sahil focused on the ball, and kicked it so hard that it flew straight into the defender's face, smashing his nose. The poor guy instantly fell to the ground, bleeding profusely. Sahil gritted his teeth out of satisfaction as he walked over to where the crowd had gathered around the injured player, and expressed his fake concern before walking away. Julie, who was amongst the audience had watched all of this, and was beginning to get worried about the new Sahil that she was noticing.

He started winning at every sport that he participated in including swimming, basketball, athletics, etc. And the more he won, the more addicted he got to the high. Being the number one pick for school sports teams intoxicated him further, and his confidence had begun to turn into arrogance.

Sahil began to lose interest in studies, which reflected in his rapidly slipping grades. Julie tried to talk sense into him more than just once. However, his mind was too focused on finding innovative ways of cheating rather than studying. All his teachers, especially Mrs. Pontford started sensing a complete change in Sahil's attitude. It upset her deeply to see her star student spiral down the wrong path so quickly.

There was someone else Sahil had rubbed the wrong way too, but for completely different reasons. As Sahil's popularity amongst the Oakwoodians rose, so did Rana's jealousy towards him. He couldn't digest the fact that a junior had acquired a rockstar like status within months of walking into Oakwood. And his girlfriend Tina's sudden fondness towards Sahil made things worse. But not one to let it pass, Rana was waiting patiently for the right opportunity to strike, hard.

Chapter 42

The academic year had almost come to an end. Fights with rival schools' boys, sports practice sessions, sorting out juniors' issues, rooftop beer drinking sessions with seniors had taken up most of Sahil's time in the last semester and a half. He started spending lesser and lesser time with Julie too, as the other parts of his life had turned more exciting than ever. He felt important and powerful, not a feeling he was familiar with until he joined Oakwood. Whether it was being the talk of the school after taking on a senior from another school, or the hysterical cheering that his swimming wins usually brought – he enjoyed every minute of the fame and popularity that came his way.

One afternoon, it was the last class for the day. The sharp school bell rang, announcing the end of the session. As the students left class one after the other, Mrs. Pontford started handing out corrected test papers to them. As Sahil went up to collect his paper, she told him to wait back. He wondered why. Lately he had been avoiding Mrs. Pontford deliberately, as he knew what she thought of his new and 'improved' personality.

She interrupted his thought with a very concerned question, *"Sahil, is everything ok with you?"*

Sahil looked around to see that they both were the only ones in class now. Mrs. Pontford was holding his paper.

He promptly answered, trying to scan the paper quickly, *"Yes ma'am everything's great."*

She stared at his paper, her worried expression turning into a thoughtful one. Sahil was now uncomfortable.

Mrs. Pontford, *"Son, do you know the story of Icarus?"*

Sahil, confused, *"No ma'am…"*

The teacher leaned against her desk as she started narrating a story to him, *"Well, in Greek mythology, Icarus was a boy who dreamt of flying in the sky. So his father, a master craftsman made wings for him out of wax and feathers. Icarus was ecstatic that he could now fly, but his father warned him not to fly too high and close to the sun. Icarus promised his father that he wouldn't fly too high and took the wings, strapped them on and flew off. Icarus loved the feeling of flight, and started soaring through the clouds amongst the birds. The higher he flew the more the loved it. Ignoring his father's advice and breaking his promise, he started soaring higher and higher, and as he got higher he got closer to the sun. Soaring in the sky, looking at the sun he felt as strong as the sun. Brimming with pride, he flew closer and closer to it. But, as he flew closer to the sun, his wings made of wax started to melt and the feathers started to fall off, and before Icarus knew it, his wings had broken down and he was falling down towards the ground faster than he flew up. Finally he fell into the sea and perished."*

Sahil, who had been intently listening to Mrs. Pontford, felt uncomfortable in his skin. He understood what she was trying to tell him. Sahil felt sick in his stomach, as he was suddenly reminded of his first day in Mrs. Pontford's class where he had impressed her with his command over the English language.

He could hardly speak as he mumbled, *"Yes ma'am, I think I've heard this story as a child."*

Mrs. Pontford handed over his test paper as she replied, *"Good, then think about it, and think about the moral of the story."*

He had scored 47%, which was an enormous descend from his previous scores in 90's. He took his paper and walked right out of the classroom, too embarrassed to even make eye contact with the teacher.

As soon as Sahil got out of class, he saw Caesar in his sports gear and remembered that they had an important football match in an hour.

Caesar, *"What the hell dude, get ready fast, its nearly time!"*

All thoughts of guilt or remorse were pushed aside immediately. Sahil went running to the dorm to get changed for the match. He was the team captain after all.

Chapter 43

The football ground at Nainital's city centre was buzzing with hundreds of uniformed students. Some of them were getting ready to perform with their drums and trumpets. Others were sitting around the field, holding up banners and boisterously shouting out the anthem of the school they were there to support. It was a crucial match. The interschool football finals were being played between Oakwood and its arch rivals, St. Edwards. The excitement and competition in the air were more prevalent today than on any other match day. The reason being, in the past 14 years both the schools had won 5 finals each. Which meant that the next 60 minutes weren't just going to help either one of the schools swoop the final victory. They were going to decide which one creates history – Oakwood or St. Edwards.

Students from both schools were there in full attendance, and both sides knew that between the two schools, 'healthy' competition was just a myth, especially at a match like today. Both the team captains came forward for the toss.

Sahil lost the toss, and St. Edwards was going to kick the game off. Slightly disappointed, Sahil who was playing defence went back to the rest of his team. All the players were directed to get on field by the commentator. The Oakwoodians fist thumped each other and yelled their unofficial motto, *'Let there be bloodshed'* before assuming their positions.

The players looked like bulls from one of the Spanish bullfights, raring to go. The whistle was blown, the WAR had begun. The centre forward from St. Edwards kicked off and the players dribbled their way past the Oakwood players. And then, one of them struck with a clean goal straight into the net. The deafening uproar from the supporters lasted for almost 10 minutes. After this for the next 20 minutes, the entire ground turned into a violent mud storm with both sides playing neck-to-neck. Along the way, Oakwood managed to scored a goal too. The whistle for half time was blown. Both sides were screaming out their respective anthems.

A whole year of practice, sweat and blood had gone into this moment and losing wasn't an option for either team. Tension was soaring and the pressure on the players was tremendous. Sahil and the team huddled up for a quick strategy discussion before getting on field for the remainder of the match. A few minutes into the 2nd half, the centre forward from St. Edwards almost scored a goal which Oakwood's goalkeeper, Mann blocked.

Up until the last 20 seconds, both teams had a number of such misses. Everyone was convinced it was going to be a draw. Sahil looked up at the scoreboard that read 1-1, before grabbing a glimpse of the audience. He noticed Julie and the other Oakwoodians going hysterical, screaming their lungs out in support of Sahil and the team. The energy in the air had an almost electric effect on Sahil who was playing defence. He turned his attention back onto the field, and decided to leave his defence position. He sprinted towards mid-field and tackled the ball away from the opponent's midfielder, swiftly dribbling it closer to the goal. And then, like a bull that had seen red, he charged full force towards the goalpost, guarding the ball so fiercely, that anyone trying to tackle him was rammed out of the way. Only when he was just 15 feet away from the goal, did he slow down to swing his foot hard. The ball shot through the goalkeeper's outstretched arms and went right into the mid of the net, announcing Oakwood's win – loud and clear.

The winning team was ecstatic as they jumped on top of each other, in celebration of their momentous victory. Oakwood's drummers and trumpeters got on field and started blaring the school's official anthem at volumes befitting a national festivity.

As the boys were rejoicing on field, suddenly a stone hit Sethi's head and he started bleeding. Sahil looked up to see a shower of stones flying across. They were coming from the students amongst the audience of the losing school's team. He was immediately concerned for Julie's safety, who was there with the rest of the players' girlfriends. Sahil ran across the field and grabbed her hand, as did the others with their respective girlfriends. The boys led the girls through the crowd, out of the ground and out of danger. They instructed them to go back to school with the younger junior students.

Chapter 44

After dropping off their girlfriends, the boys ran back on to the field. Furious, they headed in a pack towards the opponent team's audience from where the stones had come. Everyone was silent for a minute, and then came another stone, headed straight towards Sahil's face. He quickly ducked, protecting himself from the sharp rock that almost got his eye. After this, all hell broke loose.

Boys from both the schools went for each other's throats and a mini riot broke out. Neither side showed any sign of stopping, as they kept on punching each other mercilessly. Soon, a football match had taken an ugly turn and turned into a bloody battle. Bystanders had gathered around the field. However, none of them was ready to get themselves involved and risk their own wellbeing at the cost of protecting these thugs.

Luckily one of the shopkeepers who owned a shop across the ground had alerted the police station, reporting the violence. In a few minutes, the local police ran in with laathis and brought the riot under control.

Chapter 45

The news of the fight had reached Mr. Pontford even before the boys came back to school. Later that evening, an assembly was called for all the students at sharp 6 o'clock. Sahil and the rest of the team got back from the town and headed straight to the dorm bathrooms to wash up, before anyone could notice their bruised faces and blood-soiled uniforms.

The entire school had lined up in full attendance that evening. There was pin drop silence as Mr. Pontford walked into the courtyard. The serious expression on his face gave away just one thing away –whatever he was about to say or do wasn't going to be very pleasant.

The principal's stern voice echoed as he spoke. "*What happened in the city today was disgraceful, to say the least. Oakwoodians have had a history of being gentlemen, and gentlemen don't brawl on the streets like common "chokras". Let me remind all of you that as students of this school, each one of you is expected to behave with a certain amount of grace and dignity. And you all have failed miserably. This is the darkest day in the history of the school!*"

Saying this, he walked off, leaving Rudra to take over. The head boy waited patiently for Mr. Pontford to leave before he broke into a slight smirk.

"*Ok guys, I know I shouldn't be saying this, but firstly congratulations on the big win in the match today.*"

On hearing this, the entire school nearly broke out into claps. Rudra immediately hushed them down, in light of Mr. Pontford's speech. However, he didn't let the celebrations die as he continued to speak,
"*I know they started the fight, but what the hell, you'll did teach them a damn good lesson. Go, enjoy yourselves now. School dismissed!*"

Most of the boys had nasty bruises from the fight, but were elated at Rudra's little congratulatory speech. With his spirits lifted, Sahil too, started walking towards his dorm with the rest of his group when Julie went running to him and caught hold of his arm.

Chapter 46

Julie looked worried, *"Sahil I need to talk to you, come with me."*

She pulled him by the arm, leading him to a quieter corner.

Sahil, *"What's up?"*

Julie paused for a few seconds before finally speaking, *"I've been meaning to talk to you for a few days now. But I've been worried if you'd get me wrong. Anyway, I have to tell you what's on my mind cause it's eating me up inside."*

Sahil grew slightly concerned, *"What's wrong Jules? Is everything ok? Did you get hurt in the city today?"*

She studied the bruises on his face, *"No, I'm fine. But the fight today? You could have seriously been hurt. There wasn't any need to..."*

Julie broke down as she struggled to complete her sentence.

Sahil held her face, trying to comfort her as he spoke. *"Babe, relax. I'm not hurt. And all I was doing was protecting you and everyone else. They started the fight, I was just upholding the school honour!"*

Julie argued, *"No that's exactly it! There is no honour in fighting, Sahil. And it isn't just about today. Over the last few months I've been noticing a change in you and I don't know if this change is good. You just seem to be a different person from when you joined. All the rage, the pride, its not good for you darling."*

Sahil shot back, *"Yes, you know what, maybe I have changed. But this is who I am now. Do you expect me to be the naïve, frightened person I used to be? What good did that do to me? Get me beaten up all the time? Now people respect me, they like me."*

Julie was in tears as she tried to reason out with Sahil.
"No Sahil, they fear you, they don't respect you."

An agitated Sahil banged his fist on the wall they were standing next to.

"Fine let them fear me then, screw it! I don't care. Its better THEY live in fear than ME. I've bloody lived in fear all my life. Not anymore. You don't even know shit about me."

Julie held his hand, trying to calm him down.

"No I don't baby. Tell me then. I want to know."

Sahil pulled his hand away. *"You know why I was sent here? Cause my parents were getting divorced. I wasn't given a choice. I had no control over my life, and I lived in constant fear of what was going to happen next. So what happens when I come here? The first day of school itself, Rana beats me after calling me a bastard. You want me to go back to being that weak bastard whose life is a toy, being remote controlled by someone else? I'm sorry, that's not going to happen. Now people are scared of me, and they should be. Otherwise I will bloody teach them a lesson they wont forget."*

Sahil's eyes were glazed as he walked away from Julie. Everything he had been through since his childhood, everything that he wanted to forget when he came to Oakwood – it had all come flooding back in an instant. Sahil was angry with Julie for having picked on the scabs from wounds that hadn't properly healed yet. She had brought out the weak side in him. But more than her, he was angry with himself. He thought he had turned stronger. He was happy that the meek, voiceless boy who had walked through those big, red Oakwood gates was gone forever. But at that moment, he realised that the boy he had tried so hard to leave behind was still there. In fact he was right beneath the surface, and so were all the wounds that he had endured through his past. It made him feel vulnerable and powerless that one scratch and the pain had come gushing back to sting him.

Julie stood there shocked as she took in everything Sahil has just said. She had known him for almost a year, and yet she knew so less about the person he was.

Chapter 47

It had been a long day for the boys. But back at the dorm, no one showed a hint of fatigue. Everyone was in a mood to celebrate. Not just had the boys earned themselves a well-deserved victory, but the next day was Sahil's 15th birthday too. Caesar and the gang were hiding behind the dorm room door, waiting for him.

Sahil stormed into the dorm angrily, after the fight with Julie, to be greeted by his batch mates. The moment he walked in, they all flocked around him. Before he could even realise what was happening, he was up in the air being bounced around like a rock star at a concert. Some of the boys were chanting his name, while others were singing the school's sports anthem. The entire school had seen and was talking about the impressive skill he had displayed during the match. They all knew that if there was one person who was responsible for Oakwood's glorious win at the match that day, it was Sahil.

Caesar and the other boys spiritedly sang the sport anthem, "*Ole ole ole ole, we are the champions, we are the champions.*"

Sahil completely forgot about his fight with Julie as his anger quickly turned to elation. He soaked in every moment of the praise and the adulation.

Caesar raised his bottle of water, as if raising a toast. "*And the award for best sportsman of the year goes to… Mr. Sahil Madhavan. Bloody awesome game man, you killed it today, respect bro!*"

Sahil, giving his best shot at sounding humble, "*Thank you boys, but, you'll weren't too bad yourselves. No but seriously guys, we rocked as a team.*"

"*Screw all that now birthday boy! Get ready, we have a 'chew' to go to. Rudra has organised a kickass party for us. Time to get wasted!*"

Sahil was surprised that Caesar knew it was his birthday. He then realised that he had probably found out from the monthly birthday reminders list that the teachers would religiously put up in the dining hall. Excited about the party, the 'almost 15' year old went to the bathroom to freshen up. And then, he suddenly remembered. They had a marathon to run the next day, and drinking wasn't going to be the best way to prepare for it.

He ran back out to Caesar, "*Bro wasted? We have marathons tomorrow dude.*"

Caesar dismissed Sahil's concern as he put his arm on his shoulder, "*Arrey.. Thoda hi piyenge yaar (lets drink a little). Birthdays and victories don't come everyday. Chal!*"

Chapter 48

A 'chew' was a very important event in an Oakwoodian's life. It was a 'by invite only' party thrown by prefects. The only juniors that got entry into this party were the ones who had proven themselves worthy of an invitation. At a chew, there was alcohol, cigarettes, outside food – basically everything that the prefects would otherwise pull students up for, on any other day. A 'chew' happened twice or thrice a year, and was the only time the seniors and juniors mingled as equals. This was the first time Sahil was attending such a gathering. He had no idea what was going to happen there. The only thing he knew was that it was a matter of pride to be invited to one of these parties. Attending a chew was an automatic way of entering the 'it club' of Oakwood.

This time, the chew was happening in one of the 11th grade dorm rooms. On a normal day, this dorm would be out of limits even for students from 10th grade. But this was a big night for the Oakwood boys, and an exception had been made. Sahil looked around and noticed how much bigger, better furnished and cooler the dorm was compared to their 9th grade matchboxes. There were dumb bells, a music system and graffiti on the walls. There were LED lights too, that seemed to have been specially organised for the party. One of the beds had been turned into a bar, with bottles of cheap black rum stocked up with soft drinks like Limca and Thums Up next to them.

As Sahil walked into the party with Caesar and the rest of the gang, he received a welcome worthy of a homecoming king. Through the rest of the night, he was pretty much the centre of attention. Watching all the seniors recognise him and praise him for his performance earlier that day, gave him a heady high.

Suddenly, the music stopped playing. Everyone began to wonder what had gone wrong, when Rudra walked to the centre of the room. *"So guys, most of you may not know but the star of the evening is also turning a year older in a couple of hours. Let's give our boy, Sahil Madhavan, a birthday to remember guys!"* Saying this, he poured a big shot of neat rum at the makeshift bar, and got Sahil to chug it in one go. After this, the rest of the boys followed suit by indulging the birthday boy with one shot after another. By the 4rd one, Sahil had forgotten all about the marathon he was supposed to attend the next day.

Rana, who was also attending the party, watched Sahil and his friends from a distance. He smiled to himself, as suddenly he realised he had struck upon a golden opportunity for sweet revenge.

Chapter 49

The sharp twang of the school bell stung like a million nails in the boys' ears. Sahil, Caesar and the rest of the gang woke up with splitting headaches, thanks to the cheap rum from the night before. All of them looked groggy and tired as they got out of their beds. It was the first time the boys had had rum and they could all feel the after effects of the heavy binge.

None of them felt good, but Sahil especially seemed to be in a far worse condition than the rest of them. He was suddenly regretting his decision to attend that party instead of resting it out the previous night. The football match, the following fight and the heavy-duty celebration had taken its toll. His body felt sore and stiff.

However, he knew nothing much could be done now. He had no choice but to get ready and head to the marathon course for the race. He did a few stretches as if trying to compensate for the abuse he had subjected his body to the previous night, and headed out with the rest of the gang.

Chapter 50

The narrow streets of Nainital town were all blocked off for the interschool marathon that day. This was an important event that had been initiated by the Board of District of Nainital, with just a few small schools in the area.

As he reached Oakwood's assembly area, he noticed Julie standing there with her friends. While all the others walked up to him to wish him 'happy birthday', she stood awkwardly in the corner. Sahil started walking towards her, when Caesar yelled across from a distance, that the marathon was about to begin. Sahil quickly glanced over to Julie, who looked away. He had no choice but to run to the start line without meeting her.

At around 8.30 am, when they arrived, it was a pleasant, foggy morning. However, by the time the marathons started, it was 10 o'clock. The cool breezy morning had quickly made way for a hot, sunny day.

Every school in Nainital was participating. A crowd of school students in various uniforms were standing at different points, cheering for the participants along the marathon course. The students from St. Edwards were there too. But this time, the teachers from both schools as well as cops were present to ensure a peaceful gathering.

As Sahil and the rest arrived at the start line, they noticed their archrivals there. Cold stares were exchanged, and abuses were hurled under the breaths too. But before things could go any further, the gun was fired for the race to begin. They all started running at top speed, trying to get as ahead of each other as possible. Sahil and Caesar too, started sprinting in the beginning. However, soon the partying from the night before caught up, coupled with the glaring sun. Suddenly they had to stop at various points to throw up all over the track. The other schools' contestants who they had left far behind in the beginning, soon caught up. Within no time, most other runners had raced ahead and taken the lead by a good distance. Sahil and the rest of the boys struggled on as they watched the other schools' participants disappear ahead.

Finally, after a number of breaks and stumbles, Sahil and Caesar finally made it to the finish line. They knew that they were amongst the last ones to reach there. The rest of the students and teachers from Oakwood who were there to cheer the boys, looked at them disappointed.

The only one grinning was Rana. Being their prefect, he had something very special coming for them. Sahil and Caesar noticed his sadistic smile and knew that they were in trouble. The awards function for the marathon winners that went on for the next 2 hours felt like a punishment. Other than the dehydrated and sick feeling, St. Edwards sweeping almost all the winning titles made the loss unbearable.

Sahil was extremely quiet for the rest of the day. He was by far, the most disappointed amongst them all. After a long winning spree with every sport he participated in, he had forgotten what it was like to fail. And this was the first time in a while that he had had to taste the bitter taste of failure. He decided he didn't like it one bit.

Chapter 51

The boys returned to school after the marathon, tired and defeated. They had gone two days and a night with hardly any sleep or rest, and were feeling the effects of it. Their bodies were ready to give up. The only thing they wanted to do was to go back to their dorms and pass out. But as soon as they got back, a junior came running to their dorm. Sahil, Caesar and the others who had participated in the race that day had been called to the courtyard.

The boys looked at each other, clueless as to what this was all about. Without saying a word, Sahil took the lead while the rest followed him. As he and the gang walked out of the dorm and arrived at the courtyard, they noticed Rana standing there with a wily smirk on his face. Sahil walked up right in front of him, arrogantly looking the prefect in the eye.

Pleased with himself for having stayed patient, Rana's smirk turned into a grin. *"And so the screw-ups strike again! I knew I just had to wait for you'll to slip up and then I would nail you'll. Now, I could either punish you boys or I could just go and tell Mr. Pontford that you'll were drinking last night, and let him expel you."*

As Rana spoke, Sahil's initial arrogance started turning into concern. It dawned upon Sahil that Rana's threat wasn't such a farfetched idea after all. If Mr. Pontford found out that they were drinking the earlier night, there was no excuse that would save them from being expelled. Suddenly, Sahil felt blood rushing to his face and panic running through every vein of his body. He looked flushed as his dad's voice began to ring in his ears, *"I'm so proud of you son! You have been doing so well."* He felt a little faint as his bravado quickly turned to helplessness. He stared at the ground, unable to meet Rana's eyes anymore.

Rana stared at Sahil as he continued to speak, slowly, enjoying each torturous word that he uttered. *"Boys, now that I have such a predicament. I shall leave the choice up to my very good friend and today's birthday boy Sahil."* He took a long pause before he continued, *"So Mr. Madhavan, what do you suggest I do? Tell Ponty or punish you guys."*

As anger and fear, both made way, Sahil clenched his jaws hard. He didn't say a word.

"Come on Sahil, let's hear it. Cat got your tongue?" Rana kept probing.

Left with no choice, Sahil reluctantly mumbled, *"Punishment."*

"What's that? Speak loudly CHOTU, lets hear it clearly!"
Shooting a sharp look into Rana's eyes, Sahil replied firmly this time, *"Punishment!"*

"So be it 'chotu', punishment it is! You idiots are now going to know what it is to mess with me."

He went up to Sahil and held his face hard as he threatened him. *"You! You fought with me right. Think you're too strong? Lets see how you get through the night."*

Chapter 52

"Give me 100 push-ups RIGHT NOW! Come on."

Rana wasted no time beginning his merciless punishments immediately. And why wouldn't he, when he had been waiting to do this for months. But thanks to Rudra and the other seniors' growing fondness for Sahil and his gang, the right opportunity hadn't presented itself up until now.

The boys, sore in their muscles from the previous day's aftereffects, started stumbling through the fatigues almost immediately.

It was 7 pm and the bell for dinner rang. They were all starving after the day's run, but no one dared to pause. Rana showed no sympathy either, as he moved on to the next fatigue, *"Frog jumps, 50. And faster buttheads!"*

Their legs were shaking, as if ready to give way with each jump. However, everyone knew the consequences if they stopped. Sethi and another boy almost passed out, and were treated to stinging hockey stick strikes right on the butts. Hearing his friends squealing in pain, Sahil couldn't take it anymore. He almost stopped in the middle of his fatigues to argue back with Rana, when Caesar stopped him. He reminded him of the repercussions that would be, if the principal found out about the alcohol. Going through this hell seemed like a better option than to get expelled.

Sahil's 15th birthday had turned more memorable than he had imagined.

The punishments that began at around 7 pm went right up till 6 o'clock the next morning. Finally at dawn, much to the relief of the boys, Rana announced that the punishments were done. Drenched in sweat and mud, the boys could hardly even walk.

Just then, Rudra who had just gotten out for morning P.T. drill saw the boys limping back to their dorms. Just when he was about to ask them what was going on, he saw Rana walk behind them, with a grin on his face.

Chapter 53

Rudra was furious. *"What the hell is going on here?"*

Before Rana could answer, he pointed at him, *"Stay here. I'll deal with you in a bit."*

He ran over to Caesar who was almost about to collapse, and held him up.

On seeing what bad shape all the boys were in, he called out to a couple of younger students who were passing by, *"Take them to the infirmary immediately!"*

The students helped Sahil and his friends limp to the school's hospital.

Rudra turned to Rana, *"What the hell is wrong with you? You want to kill them? How dare you punish them without asking me?"*

Rana sarcastically replied, *"Well, you probably don't know but they were drinking last night. And being as kind as I was, I gave them a choice to either tell Ponty or punish them. They chose the punishment, and since drinking is so wrong I had to discipline them properly right?"* He was still grinning, not showing even a hint of remorse at the state he had left the boys in.

Rudra held him by the collar as he spoke, *"Listen to me you piece of shit. Go try to pull that off with someone else you understand? You bloody ever do that again, I won't only de-badge you, but also kick your butt personally. Don't you forget who the hell I am."*

He shoved Rana away and walked off as Rana looked on angrily.

Chapter 54

The boys went to the infirmary, hoping to be in and out of there in a few minutes. However, on seeing the boys battered, exhausted and dehydrated, the infirmary doctor refused to let them leave. He, along with the nurses immediately put them on drips and kept a close watch on their health for the next few hours.

Later that afternoon, the resident nurse of the infirmary, Nurse Golmes gave them vitamin shots and monitored their drips.

Nurse Golmes had been with the school hospital almost for 40 years. She was a pleasant lady with a nice-natured, comforting smile. She had quit her job at the local hospital to join Oakwood's infirmary. Nurse Golmes loved children, and didn't have any of her own. Having lost her husband at a very young age during the pre-independence era, she had dedicated her life to this school and its students. Her healing powers were in her motherly touch that seemed to work wonders. Especially for these school children who were away from home for months.

As the 70 year old walked over to Sahil, the sound of her footsteps immediately woke him up. He tried to sit up. But a sharp throbbing sensation shot down his back, making it impossible to do anything but lie back down again. As he collapsed in pain, Nurse Golmes tried to hold him in a comfortable position.

"Just relax, don't try to get up. You are going to have to let your body recover over the next couple of days."

Sahil jumped up again, this time the shooting pain causing him to fall back onto the bed. All he could manage was to squawk as he tried to ignore his aching back. *"Couple of days? We have our interschool competitions going on, we can't be here for a couple of days!"*

Unaffected by the plea, Nurse Golmes calmly smiled, *"Well, you don't really have a choice here, you'll were severely dehydrated and have muscle injuries. Besides, the condition you'll are in, you'll aren't going to win any competition."*

Chapter 55

The next day were the interschool marathon finals and the streets were still blocked off for the runners. A crowd of school students were standing at various points along the course to cheer for the participants, just like on the earlier day. Having won most of the prizes the previous day, the students participating in the finals were mostly Edwardites. The only runners from Oakwood were the girls, as none of the boys had even been allowed to step out of the school hospital.

It was the end of the marathon finals and once again, St. Edwards dominated the winning positions at the prize distribution ceremony. The daylong event went on till 5 pm. Everyone was tired, and the Oakwoodians were especially low on spirit. They had all heard of the gruelling punishments Rana had subjected Sahil and his friends to. As the crowd started dispersing, Julie started walking away too. She looked visibly upset as she chose to walk alone to school, leaving the rest of the girls behind.

Rana noticed this, and his wicked mind started working in more wrong ways than one. The rest of his group too spotted Julie, and decided to grab this opportunity. They were 5-6 of them. All of them surrounded her like hungry wolves, and started teasing her.

Rana grabbed her hand, "*Hey Julie! Since your boyfriend isn't around, why don't I fill in for him?*"

Julie was shocked at this lewd comment by a fellow Oakwoodian. She stood there for a few seconds, just staring at him, disgusted. She quickly snapped back to her senses and pulled her arm away in fear. She realised she wasn't close enough either to school to be able to run to the gates, nor to the town where she could cry out for help.

It was getting dark, and Julie started panicking. Just as she tried to escape from Rana and his friends, he grabbed her arm again. This time he held it so hard, that it started getting numb. Julie struggled to free herself, as Rana just laughed, "*Don't be scared. I can take care of you better than he ever did. Want me to come to your dorm?*"

Traumatised, the poor girl attempted to pull her arm away with all her force, and fell to the ground. She broke into tears as she got up and dusted her clothes, before trying to get away again. This time too, Rana's friends blocked her path, making it impossible for Julie to escape. Looking at her struggle to break away from their clutches, the boys broke out into loud villainous laughter. The more she pleaded with them to let her go, the louder their guffaws turned.

Suddenly, out of nowhere, Tina walked in and slapped Rana hard. She was red with rage as she held Julie and walked away. Rana and his friends immediately backed off. Before a shell-shocked Rana could say a word, Julie ran towards school, sobbing. Tina stormed off after her.

That night, Julie cried uncontrollably while Tina just sat in bed and stared into oblivion. She was still stunned by Rana's behaviour. She couldn't believe she had been with such a demon for the last 2 years. Hadn't she seen the signs? Each time he punished the juniors, hadn't she noticed the pleasure he got out of it? Or had she turned a blind eye all this while, for the sake of the power and perks that came along with being a prefect's girlfriend?

Chapter 56

The boys were finally deemed fit to be discharged by the infirmary doctor. Seventh grader Rahul, who was unofficially known as 'khabari' (informer) for his resourcefulness on the latest happenings at Oakwood, came running across the courtyard. It was 8.30 in the morning. Most other students had just finished their breakfast, and were stepping out of the mess. On seeing the 'khabari' excitedly running towards the courtyard, they all stopped to find out what information he brought.

Excited, Rahul yelled loud enough for the entire crowd to hear, *"They are back. Sahil and the gang have been discharged!"*

No sooner had he finished delivering the news, than Sahil and the gang walked into the courtyard. They were immediately swarmed by their friends from every grade, wanting to catch up on everything that the boys had been through in the last few days. By now, everyone had heard about the sadistic fatigues that Rana had subjected them to. And automatically, Sahil and his friends turned into heroes once again in the eyes of the rest of the students for going through the fatigues like men. Rana on the other hand, was once again the most hated entity at Oakwood.

As Sahil caught up with his batch mates, he saw Julie walking at the far end with her friends. He realised that he hadn't spoken to her after their fight, the evening before the marathon. Eager to see her, he went running towards her. Julie noticed Sahil coming towards her, and quickly increased her pace in an attempt to avoid him. Sahil caught up anyway.

Puzzled, he held her hand, *"Where are you off to babe? You didn't even notice me."*

Julie pulled her hand away, and started walking off without saying a word. Confused with this behaviour, Sahil grabbed her hand again. Her friends quietly walked away, sensing that the couple needed a moment in private.

"You still angry about that fight? It's been a week since we've spoken babe. Chill na. I'm sorry."

Julie suddenly broke down at how casually Sahil wanted her to 'chill' and forget about everything.

"Hey, hey, hey, why are you crying? Come on stop. I won't fight again ok, sorry. Come on stop babe."

Finally, Julie gathered herself and decided to clear the air.

"I can't be with you anymore Sahil. It's over."
Their relationship hadn't been the same in the past weeks. But Sahil had been so consumed with the fame and popularity that had suddenly come his way, that it had driven Julie away. And sadly, he hadn't even realised it.

"What?" Sahil was stunned at this drastic decision that Julie had taken.

"I'm breaking up with you Sahil."

"What the hell are you talking about?"

"Sahil, please don't make this harder for me than it already is. We just can't be together."

"Why? Because of one bloody fight that I had? Are you serious?", he questioned her arrogantly.

"No Sahil, its not that. It isn't just that one fight. Don't you get it? You have changed. You are not the person I fell in love with. You are too consumed with your pride and your newfound power, and I really don't like the new YOU that you so want to be. In fact I despise the new you, and the Sahil I fell in love with, would also have despised what you have become. You have become exactly what you hated – the violence that you once hated is now festering in you. And I can't be a part of any of this."

Sahil, who had been listening to her, had tears in his eyes as she spoke. Julie took something out of her backpack and gave it to him, before walking away. It was a gift he had given her a few months back. Too shocked to react, he didn't say a word.

As Julie left, a tear rolled down Sahil's cheek. Whether he admitted it or not, he knew deep within that every word of what she had said was true. He had pushed Julie away by taking her for granted.

Chapter 57

As Julie walked away to the girl's hostel, Sahil stood there staring at the four-leaf clover that she had just returned.

Sahil had found this rare clover on their first date together, on the way back to school from Nainital town. In fact, it had marked the beginning of their relationship. Since that day, Julie had kept it safe and treasured in her English Literature textbook. He remembered her telling him that this clover was a symbol of their relationship that was based on faith, hope, love and luck. It was luck that had brought him to Oakwood, love that had brought them together, faith that got them through the tough times and hope that made her believe in them despite all the ups and downs. And she had returned it to him, just like that. Within a moment, everything had changed. Sahil knew he couldn't blame Julie for breaking up with him. In fact, when he looked back at the last few months, he realised how badly he had treated her. He felt very guilty, but it was too late. The damage had been done.

Over the next few days, he stayed aloof and distant. No amount of cheering or joking with his friends was able to put Sahil out of his misery. Even in class, he would be distracted by Julie's presence. It wasn't easy being around her, and yet not being able to be with her or even talk to her. He felt helpless. Every time he mustered the courage to go up to her and apologise, she would walk away. Sethi, Caesar and his friends were beginning to get concerned about Sahil. He had been this way for more than 2 weeks, and had shown no sign of recovering from the heartbreak.

Rana on the other hand, was enjoying watching Sahil in pain.

Chapter 58

One day after the last class for the day was over, Sahil stayed back in class. He was lagging behind on some of his assignments for the final submissions, and was trying to catch up on them. Tina noticed Sahil sitting alone and came over to him.

"Sahil, I need to tell you something."

This was the first time that they had spoken after she had dumped him for Rana, during Sahil's first week at Oakwood. Which is why, when she walked up to him, he was taken aback.

Sahil looked at her, confused, *"What?"*

She hesitated for a moment before she continued, *"When you were admitted in the infirmary, after the marathon finals, Rana and his friends harassed Julie..."*

She narrated the entire incident to him. She told him about how Rana and his gang had surrounded Julie, and how she had found her at the right moment. As she recounted the details, it all flashed in front of Sahil's eyes as if it was happening at that very moment.

Tina assured him that no harm had been caused to Julie, but what Sahil had heard had been enough to send him into a fit of rage. His eyes had turned red with anger by the time she finished telling him the whole story.

What Rana had done to him and his friends might have been cruel. But how he had behaved with Julie was not something that could be 'sorted' out with just a fight or altercation. That's when Sahil decided – Rana had crossed the boundary from humanity to becoming an animal, and he had to be dealt with as one.

Chapter 59

Sahil stormed back to his dorm with a deadly look in his eyes. Caesar and the gang were sitting by the window. He walked up to them and told them all that had happened in their absence. The boys were enraged too, and immediately decided that revenge had to be taken.

There was only one rule amongst the boys here at Oakwood. No matter how ugly it got between them, no matter how many abuses were hurled or how much blood was shed, no one was to EVER involve the girls. And Rana and his gang had taken it way beyond just involving them.

Still shaking with anger, Sahil announced, "*Guys, ever since my first day Rana's been after me. And after what I heard today, I've had enough. It is time to finally end this.*"

They all agreed.

Chapter 60

That night, neither Sahil nor his friends slept at lights out. They let a good 15 minutes pass after the lights went off to see if any of the other prefects were doing the rounds. Then, they got out of bed and sneaked out of the dorm without waking anyone up.

Rana, who always fancied a late night snack, usually snuck into the dining room for some leftover grub from dinner. The boys knew about this habit of his, and devised a plan accordingly.

Even that night, a few hours post dinner, the boys had seen Rana walking towards the dining room. Knowing that he would be out in around ten minutes, they waited patiently. He was all by himself as walked back out of the dining room and headed towards the loo. Suddenly, a blanket was thrown over him. It was Sahil and the boys. Two of them held Rana tight as he tried to struggle and Caesar held his mouth shut so he doesn't shout and wake anyone up. Sahil clutched both his feet, making sure he doesn't escape. Together, they carried him to the back of the school that overlooked a cliff. The only thing separating the school and the pitch-black abyss that the cliff overlooked was a rundown brick wall. Sahil glanced over the wall with a cold, dead expression on his face. His friends looked at him for approval. As soon as he nodded, they threw Rana off the cliff. As the boys stared down at the valley cradling the small Nainital town, neither of them showed any fear or regret at what they had just done. After a few moments, Sahil looked down, satisfied with the retribution he had dealt. Through his clenched teeth, he let every word echo in his head as he spoke, *"See you in hell!"*

Remorseless, Sahil and his friends walked away.

It had been almost a year since he had walked through those gates of Oakwood, incapable of hurting even a moth. And today, he had turned into a monster that didn't flinch even at the thought of killing a fellow student.

Chapter 61

This year at Oakwood had been an adventure for the entire gang. But it hadn't taken much time for this thrilling adventure to turn into a nightmare. From leaking exam papers to picking fights to sneaking into the girl's hostel - the boys had a laundry list of unfavourable things they had done in the past one year. But murder hadn't been one of them, yet.

That night, Sahil and his friends went to their locker room. They had smuggled in some bottles of beer, like they usually did. But the mood was very different tonight. Everyone sat quiet, sipping on the alcohol and passing the bottle around.

As Caesar took the last sip of the beer, he looked worried. He toyed around with the bottle, staring at it as he spoke.

"Shucks man, you think he really is dead? I mean, I think we went too far. Killing someone isn't right man. I have this visual of his parents crying at his funeral and I just can't get it out of my head."

Mann, who was sitting right next to him, jumped in as if waiting for someone to talk about it.

"Yeah man! We really shouldn't have thrown him off. Do you think we should go and check if he's alive?"

Everyone else too, agreed that in a fit of rage, they had gone to too much of an extreme to teach Rana a lesson. Sahil was the only one who seemed unfazed. He didn't have even a hint of regret or shame on his face. Just as they opened another bottle of beer, the boys heard a thundering of shouts accompanied by footsteps coming towards them. Before they could realise what was happening, they saw a group of at least 30 seniors charge at them. They all surrounded Sahil and his friends and started beating them up with hockey sticks. It was just the six of them against about thirty seniors.

Five of the senior boys took turns kicking and punching Sahil. While one kicked him in the groin, another hit him in the face. And then, another big built guy delivered a full-on blow into Sahil's back, bringing him straight to the floor. As he lay on the floor, trying to regain his strength to fight back, he noticed Rana walking towards him. His clothes were tattered and muddy, possibly caused by the struggle while he climbed back up the steep cliff. Rana didn't die from the fall after all. He had minor bruises and scratches on his arms and face, but otherwise he was alive and kicking!

Furious, he walked towards Sahil who was already on the floor, and kicked him in the stomach. Sahil squirmed with pain, but that didn't stop Rana from kicking him repeatedly. In fact even the rest of the boys joined the prefect as he kept striking the 15 year old, till he started spitting up blood. As Sahil lay on the ground, writhing in agony, he noticed a hockey stick lying a few feet away. He used all his strength to stretch out and reach the stick. And before anyone could realise what he was up to, he picked it up and jumped to his feet. Then in one swift action, Sahil delivered a full blow into one of the seniors' heads. The guy collapsed to the ground instantly. Sahil then moved on to the next senior, and then the next, beating them up ruthlessly with the hockey stick. He saw his friends still getting beaten up and started fending senior after senior off of them too.

Rana saw this and started moving backwards into the crowd. He began to run, trying to protect himself from getting thrashed like the others. Sahil immediately noticed this and chased him out of the dorms and down the stairs. He caught up with Rana within no time, and hit him in the leg with the bloody hockey stick he had in his hand. The prefect tripped over the next step and fell down into the front courtyard.

By now, the ruckus had woken up the entire school that had gathered around, curious to see what was happening. Rana was down on the floor, trembling. He tried to get up a few times, but each time Sahil would smash the hockey stick into his leg, bringing him back to the ground, and finally breaking his leg.

An animalistic rage had taken over Sahil. He threw the hockey stick away and started punching Rana. The senior slipped into semi-consciousness, as Sahil sat on his chest and continued to throw punch after punch into his bloody face. He didn't realise how badly he had beaten up Rana, till there was a loud yell that snapped him out of this mad fit. He stopped immediately and turned around to look. It was the principal standing there, shocked at what he was seeing. He was staring at Sahil whose clothes, hands, neck and even face we covered in blood... Rana's blood.

Since he had heard about Rana's attack on Julie, a maddening, trance-like violence had taken over Sahil, allowing him to do the things he had done in the past few hours. The Principal's voice had finally brought Sahil back to his senses. Sahil stared at his hands and clothes covered in blood. He felt disgusted at himself, rather than feeling powerful about having won a fight against a deadly senior like Rana. For the first time, he was ashamed of what he had become. And then it suddenly hit him. There was no difference left between Rana and him.

Mr. Pontford stared at Sahil, appalled. He was so sickened by what he had seen at his school today, that he silently asked Sahil to report to his office the next day and walked off.

Chapter 62

The next morning, Sahil was in the Principal's office, cleaned up and changed. He looked around while he stood there waiting for Mr. Pontford. He was nervous, as he knew that the punishment for what he had just done wasn't going to be a lenient one. But even through the nervousness, he couldn't stop thinking about his first day at school. Almost a year back, his journey at Oakwood had started at exactly the same place where he was standing right now.

He vividly remembered Mr. Pontford dressed in crisp grey trousers and a blue double-breasted blazer, looking every bit the title on his door. His style had been impeccably British. Sahil remembered how he had been conscious of how he was dressed, compared to the perfection that Mr. Pontford was. The principal had noticed this and had told him, *"Don't worry son, by the time you're out of Oakwood, you'll be every bit the man you have set out to be."*

Sahil had a smile on his face as he remembered that day. Just then, Mr. Pontford walked in, as impeccably dressed as the first day. But this time, he didn't have the same things to say to Sahil. He walked over to his desk with some papers, and signed them before turning to look at the teenager. As he spoke, weighing each word carefully, there was an austere yet distant tone in his voice.

"You are expelled. Here are your leaving papers. Remember I told you that you were a bad influence. Well you have proved me right today. You have disgraced this institution and everything it stands for. I have never seen any student fall as low as you. You may leave now. The school car will take you to Delhi, from where you will take a flight to Mumbai. You father has been informed."

Having said this, Mr. Pontford walked up to the door and opened it for Sahil to leave. Stunned at this news that had struck him like lightning, the 15 year old turned around and walked out blankly. He knew he was going to get a harsh punishment, but even in his wildest dreams he hadn't thought that he would ever be 'expelled' from a school.

On Sahil's way out of the office, the Principal handed over the school leaving papers to him. Unable to even look Mr. Pontford in the eye, the teenager walked out without saying a word.

Chapter 63

On his way back to the dorm, Sahil walked as slowly as his body would allow him to. Little had he known that the shy and introverted boy who had arrived at the Oakwood gates a year back, would be walking out of the same gates, guilty of violence and misconduct. He tried to remember that exact moment when everything had changed so drastically for him. He couldn't. So far he hadn't even thought of how his father was going to react to what had happened at school. But now, as he walked back and began to think of his life beyond those brick red gates, it suddenly came him. This year away from each other had strangely brought them closer than they had ever been. For the first time, Sahil had heard his father say that he was proud of him. These letters had become some kind of a sacred means of communication between them. They had opened up to each other in this one year, more than they had in their entire lifetimes. There was a stitch in Sahil's heart. He thought of the probability that things would go back to the way they used to be. In fact after hearing about his expulsion, things were most likely to get worse than they had ever been. Would he be furious or disappointed? Or would he understand him?

Before Sahil could answer his own questions, his long walk to the dorm was over. Caesar, Sethi and the rest of his friends were anxiously waiting to know what hell Mr. Pontford had brought down upon him.

Sahil walked past them, and to his bed without saying a word. He pulled out his leather suitcase from under the bed. Caesar and the gang ran behind him and snatched the papers from his hand. The boys were numbed with shock as they saw the papers were actually Sahil's 2-page expulsion letter, addressed to his father.

Caesar was furious at this harsh reaction by Mr. Pontford. *"Bro! This is unfair. He had started it! And why should you be the only one getting expelled. We were all in it together. Even we should be expelled."* Saying this, he stormed out the dorm door towards the Principal's office. Sahil rushed to him, forbidding him from doing anything stupid. He asked Caesar to promise him that he would finish his time at Oakwood. After a lot of convincing, Caesar reluctantly agreed. Trying to make things lighter, Sahil jokingly asked him to carry on his legacy at the school.

Both of them walked back to the dorm, where their friends were waiting. Sahil started packing his things into the trunk. The mood was sombre that morning. But the boys made it a point to lighten the spirit by cracking jokes and reminiscing about the fun adventures they had had together. Having friends around helped. Especially when Sahil didn't consider them as just friends. They had become family.

The last thing left for him to pack was his crisply ironed school uniform. He picked it up and looked at it for a minute, before putting it in and locking his trunk up. The news about Sahil's exit had spread across Oakwood within minutes. Everyone, right from his entire batch, to juniors who looked up to him, to seniors and even prefects had gathered outside the dorm to bid him farewell.

Sahil started to leave his dorm with his luggage. As he reached the entrance, he turned back to get one last look. As soon as he stepped out, he noticed the number of people who had turned up just to say bye and had a lump in his throat. He hugged all of his friends – batch mates, juniors and seniors, and walked out of the dorm building. As he stepped into the courtyard, he saw his favourite teacher, Mrs. Pontford waiting for him. Unable to hold in his emotions any longer, his eyes welled up with tears. As he stood in front of her, looking down, a tear rolled down his cheek.

Mrs. Pontford looked at him with a calming smile on her face. She wiped off his tear as she cleared her throat to speak, *"Now is not the time to cry son, now is the time to be stronger than you ever have. You have made mistakes but don't regret them, learn from them. Everybody has their own path and so do you. I still believe in you, I know your path will only lead you to success someday. Just hold your head up high and make wiser decisions from today, so that someday I can say with pride that he was my student. I wish you all the luck and success going ahead son, and when you do attain that success, remember what this old lady had said to you – I BELIEVE IN YOU."*

Sahil broke down and hugged her. He touched her feet and walked away, without looking back. As she saw him leave the courtyard, she took her glasses off and wiped the tears off her eyes as well.

Chapter 64

With his backpack on the shoulder and trunk in his hand, Sahil took his last stroll out of Oakwood. 'The last mile', he thought to himself. The sound of the dried leaves crushing below his feet reminded him of his first walk at Oakwood.

As he walked through the beautiful forest pathway, he suddenly felt like the nervous 14-year old who had walked in, clutching onto his Gameboy. He had been as hesitant to step into the strange world called Oakwood then, as he was to step into the world outside now.

Oakwood had become home, the only place where he had ever felt like he belonged. And now he wondered if there would be any other place in the outside world that would feel like home.

This feeling reminded him once again of a prison film he had once watched, where prisoners got so used to living in prison that they found it difficult to settle into the real, free world outside. In such cases, the prisoners often missed the security that the confines of the jail provided them with, thus committing crimes intentionally, just to be sent back to prison. Strangely he could now, somehow relate to this.

Sahil was so consumed by these thoughts that he didn't realise he had already reached the gates. There he saw Caesar, Sethi, Mann and the rest of his group already waiting for him. They smiled, each of them trying their best to conceal how distraught they were. After exchanging numbers and addresses, and making promises to see each other on the next holiday, Sahil's friends helped him load his bags in the car.

This was it. The time had come to say their final goodbyes. Everyone was quiet, trying to put off the moment for as later as they could. Sahil, of all the people knew that there was no easy way to say a goodbye. He stepped forward to hug Jatin, and the rest of them jumped in. It suddenly felt less like a farewell, and more like one of their usual huddles before their football matches.

Too choked with emotion to say any more, Sahil finally got into the car. He signalled the driver to drive off, while his friends looked on with teary eyes. As the car rolled out of the narrow pathway, Sahil kept his gaze fixed on his friends. Suddenly, he noticed someone come running from behind the boys. It was Julie. She had reached there a minute too late. Sahil turned around to look back at her from the rear windscreen of the car. They waved out to each other, both their eyes glistening with tears. He knew going back to say bye to her would make things even more difficult than they already were for both of them.

Sahil saw his school, his friends and Julie through the rear-view mirror, fading into a distance, before completely disappearing.

His time at Oakwood might have taught him the intoxicating nature of power, the use of violence and how fighting back was the only option sometimes. But it had also taught him how it was important in life to enjoy the road ahead rather than to keep revisiting the past. And that's exactly what he decided to do as he turned his eyes onto the winding roads ahead, leading out of Nainital.

Chapter 65

It was a pleasant summer morning, and the laidback town of Nainital was just waking up. Shops were opening up, the aroma of morning 'adrakwali chai' (ginger tea) being prepared at tea stalls was in the air, restaurants were putting freshly fried bhujiya-pakodas (snacks) out on display in an attempt to lure potential customers.

Suddenly, the thundering from a convoy of black SUVs woke the quaint town out of its tranquil morning routine. The cars circled around the city centre a few times, before racing off into the narrow by-lane with a road sign that read: *"Oakwood College – 1 km"*.

Within minutes, the cars had arrived at gates that read 'Oakwood College' in bold, black font. The brick red gates had made way for red glossy ones, and the watchman's wooden hut had transformed into a hi-tech bulletproof cabin with security guards that communicated through walkie-talkies. After some verification, the automatic gates opened, allowing the convoy to drive in.

As the fleet reached the entrance of the front courtyard, a team of armed men stepped out of the rest of the cars and walked towards one of them. One of them opened the car door cautiously, allowing a 30-something year old to step out. Clad in a slick business suit and an expensive pair of sunglasses, the youngster hurried into the front courtyard. He realised he was late for Oakwood's Annual Founders' Day. He ran over to the side reserved for teachers and alumni, trying his best not to disturb the on-going speech along the way.

"...That was the day I was expelled from school, and I'd made a mess of things".

As soon as the suit-clad gentleman in the audience heard this, he looked up and smiled. He realised his best friend from 20 years back, Sahil Madhavan, was the one at the podium.

Sahil paused to acknowledge his friend and dorm-mate, Caesar Rathi. After all, it had been 20 years since they had said their goodbyes at the gates of Oakwood.

Sahil went on to finish his speech that hundreds of uniform-clad Oakwoodians were intently listening to,

"People are just the sum of their experiences, some good and others bad. However, all these experiences and mistakes make us who we are. I made mine but never regretted them. I learnt from them. And those experiences, mistakes and failures make me who I am today – a better, richer person from the inside, and I wouldn't change any of it.
Mrs. Pontford was right, I still had it in me and I did change my life around. My school, Oakwood and my teacher were the best things that happened to me. It moulded me into who I am. So remember, no matter how bad a situation you are going through, it's only temporary. It will be over soon, and it will teach you something and make you stronger. There is hope. Live with that hope cause I BELIEVE in all of you, just the way Mrs. Pontford believed in me".

Sahil was the Chief Guest at Oakwood's Annual Founders' Day that year.

He was now a successful film director, and was being felicitated by the school for his accomplishment in the field of entertainment.

THE END

www.ingramcontent.com/pod-product-compliance
Lightning Source LLC
Chambersburg PA
CBHW030542130626
46552CB00006B/2377